WHEN LOVE LEADS YOU HOME

Jami Crumpton
and
Carla Rossi

Interior format by The Killion Group
http://thekilliongroupinc.com

JAMI'S DEDICATION
For my mom, who believes in me so much, I believe in myself.

CARLA'S DEDICATION
For Denise

ACKNOWLEDGEMENTS
Much love to our families for their
continued support of our writing endeavors.
Thanks to our critique partner, Stacey A. Purcell,
and our author friends at
Northwest Houston RWA and Critique Corner.

Welcome to Cardinal Point, Texas.

Where the broken find comfort,
the prodigals find peace,
and the wanderers find home.

And… you just might see a cardinal.

"Some people believe cardinals represent loved ones who have passed on. They believe the birds show up when you need comfort or confirmation. They are a sign. A remembrance. They are your loved ones visiting you, checking in on you."
Cole Boudreaux

ONE

"Ma'am, this card was declined."

"Oh… um…" Jacey Steele fumbled with her wallet and withdrew another credit card. "Try this one." She tapped her nail on the convenience store counter. Hot dog fumes and stale cigarette smoke assaulted her nose, causing her stomach to churn. Heat prickled her neck and cheeks. Every heartbeat pulsed in her head, each one stronger than the next. If she stroked out in front of the frozen drink machine and powdered donuts display, she was going to be furious.

Of course, the store was full of people to witness her humiliation. She could feel their judgey eyes boring into her back.

The breath whooshed from her lungs when the credit card machine whirred. Her knees wobbled at the sight of the white receipt curling from the device. The pimply-faced kid behind the register tore off the slip of paper. Jacey wanted to snatch it from his hand and sign before the credit fairies changed their minds. Instead, she smiled, nodded to the clerk, and carefully wrote her name with her head held high. Because even though she'd lost her livelihood and her reputation, she would cling to her last tattered shred of pride.

The phone buzzed as she slid into the car. "Meredith, please tell me you have good news."

"I don't have any news, Jacey. The investigation is ongoing, Tara's family hasn't withdrawn their suit, and the university hasn't rescinded your suspension. Same as when you left Florida. I was calling to see if you made it to Texas."

Not the call she wanted from her attorney. She'd used all her savings to put Meredith Sanders, northern Florida's best civil attorney, on retainer and she calls to make sure the GPS is working. Jacey reigned in her irritation. "Yes, I've arrived in Cardinal Point and I'm on my way to my aunt's lawyer's office to pick up the key." She waited at a stop sign for a couple of teenagers to cross the street. "Then I'll head to the bed and breakfast."

"Will Mr. Boudreaux be there as well?"

"No. I doubt I'll see him. He probably can't leave the nursing home." Jacey peered at the street sign that was partially covered by a giant wisteria bush.

"So the co-heir of the B&B is elderly?"

"With a name like Virgil Coleman Boudreaux he's got to be eighty if he's a day. Which is good. He probably doesn't have the energy to deal with the sale of the B&B, so I can handle it myself."

The sooner, the better.

"Let me know how it goes."

"I doubt I'll do that, Meredith. You're my attorney. We should keep our relationship strictly professional. There's no need to check up on me. Only call me with news as it pertains to my case."

"Pardon me for being concerned about you, Jacey. It won't happen again."

The line went dead.

"Some people are so touchy, Moe."

She scratched her terrier mutt behind the ears. The dog indulged her for a moment then turned his head away.

"I was mean, wasn't I?"

The dog eye-balled her over his shoulder. His chocolate-brown gaze clearly stated an annoyed *ya think*?

"Why am I so relationally stunted?" She glanced at the dog. "Don't answer that. We both know why."

Take a homeschooled kid, thirty-plus hours of gymnastics a week, and add in a father who alienated her from her teammates. Do that for the better part of ten years, and the result is someone with very few social skills.

She grabbed her phone and pulled up her contacts.

"Hello."

"Meredith, I'm sorry. I was rude. I appreciate you checking on me. It was very thoughtful."

Great. She sounded like she was reading from a script.

"Jacey?"

"Yes, Meredith, it's me."

"That was… unexpected and very nice. Apology accepted."

"OK… so, bye."

The dog laid his head on her lap and gave a little sigh. She rubbed his back. "You were right, Moe-

Moe. I should listen to you more often. You're better with people than I am."

Following the GPS, she made her way into the center of Cardinal Point. "Get a load of this…"

The whole place looked like a Dickens Christmas. Giant red bows adorned lamp posts lining the main drag. In the middle of town, lovely Victorian buildings framed both sides of weathered brick streets. Twinkle lights dressed decorative a-frame gables and winked from inside frosted glass storefronts and cozy tea room cafés. Huge boughs of garland looped from building to building and around the top of the courthouse. Christmas trees with red and green plaid ribbon stood like toy soldiers in front of every business.

At the traffic light, she took a moment to take it all in.

A woman walked by with a large bag of caramel corn. Jacey's taste buds yearned for the salty-sweet treat. All around, people talked and laughed as they strolled from store to store. The storybook scene before her was lovely and magical, even in the daylight.

The shop on the corner was a toy store. The spray-on snow frost and soft blinking lights showcased dolls displayed in the window. Some stood, some rested on furniture, and one was posed in an arabesque. If this didn't look like Santa's workshop, she didn't know what did.

"Oh, look, Moe. There's one in a high chair."

She'd always wanted a doll, but her father never indulged such trivial desires. All her Christmas gifts were the same for as long as she could remember: books, leotards, and a new piece of gymnastics equipment. By the time an injury forced her retirement, they had a mini-gym set up in their massive garage.

After she opened her presents on Christmas morning, her father would either set up the new equipment or retreat to his office. Snow angels, hot chocolate, and new toys were other kids' memories, not hers. She didn't mind the gifts, but what she really wanted was to do small things with her father. The only time they connected was when she earned near-perfect scores. A medal merited her a smile and a brief hug.

Remembrances of her lonely childhood and her win-at-all-cost father came crashing down on her.

Now, the cheerful holiday scene only intensified her loneliness. Pain lanced her chest as she observed the muted interactions of the townspeople from behind the car's window. The story of her life, watching, longing, hoping to be a part, to have people to care about and who cared about her, but it never happened. Bitterness oozed from the wound the pain inflicted. The only person to check up on her was an attorney she'd hired to care.

She dragged her gaze from the out-of-reach fairytale.

The computerized voice brought her back to reality as the light turned green. Her destination was less than a mile away. She shook off her melancholy and concentrated on following the directions.

Good thing she owned half of a bed and breakfast. At the very least she would have a free place to sleep tonight.

Hopefully.

CʒൠꝎ

Cole Boudreaux dropped his keys by his laptop on the old metal desk and tossed his hat onto the rack in the corner. "I like what you've done with the place."

His friend and business partner, Shane Calfee, leaned back in his rolling chair. "Hey, it's not a page out of *Office Space Beautiful* but it'll do. Your desk all right there?"

Cole surveyed the room. Cardinal Point Security Services had come a long way from his grandpa's garage. The small building they'd constructed on the adjacent lot had the basic comforts—toilet, microwave, sink, coffee pot—and he didn't have to worry about backing his chair into a riding mower or a gas can. "It's good."

He nudged a stack of orange traffic cones out of his way and found the office supplies he slid off his desk and into a box for the move across the yard. And by office supplies, he meant two pens, a phone charger, and a yellow legal pad he picked up at the rec center. With all that and his Army insignia glass paperweight, he figured he had all he needed. As for the stack of documents from the attorney, he placed those in the top drawer and shoved the warped thing closed with more effort than it should take to close a drawer. If he didn't have to look directly at them, maybe the pain of Winnie's passing would lessen.

No such luck.

Shane drummed a pen against the side of his coffee cup as he finished a call. There was silence after that, but Cole knew the conversation was about to start.

There were good and practical reasons for placing themselves face-to-face like in TV detective dramas and old-school newspaper writer rooms. For one, it kept them from losing important notes between their crappy desktops. More importantly, it allowed him to see Shane as they talked. With a hearing loss of seventy-five percent in one ear and fifty percent in the other—thank you, IED—lip reading was a necessity. His near-total deafness couldn't ever be a reason they lost or messed up a job.

Shane started drumming again. His chest heaved with a long sigh and he added a grunting sound.

Better put him out of his misery before he strained himself. "You need something?"

"Yeah, you know I do. How'd the meeting go? Are you OK?"

"Which meeting? The one about the personal security class with the Silver Foxes? Or the one with my sign language tutor?" He palmed the paperweight and then set it back down. "Or the one with that lawyer?"

"You know which one."

Cole scooted his laptop back and scrubbed his hands through his hair. "It was fine. I guess. I don't know." He stood and headed for the coffee pot. "Winnie's been gone a week. Buried three days ago, and I'm sitting in a lawyer's office and he's telling me Winnie left me half the B&B. That's all. I own half a B&B with someone I didn't know existed. Some relative Winnie never mentioned in all the years I knew her. All the years I cut her grass as a kid and drank lemonade on her porch. All the times she dragged me to church, all the letters and care packages she sent to Afghanistan. And not once while she was being the mother I didn't have, did she ever say she had real family out there somewhere."

"You were the same as family to her, Cole."

"Yeah, but to leave me half the B&B? Her blood relatives should have that." He set the pot on the warmer and reached for the sugar. "She didn't even give any clear instruction of what she wanted done with it."

"What did the lawyer say to do?"

"Apparently, the niece was as surprised as I was. He's expecting her today or tomorrow, but there'd been no sign of her when I went by. I guess she'll be here sometime to figure it out."

"What do you want to do?"

"Winnie loved that old house, and she loved taking care of people. I feel like she'd want it to stay open, but it's not like I can run it. I already have a business I'm trying to get off the ground."

He wandered to the window and caught the faint twinkle of Christmas lights around a mailbox down the street. Winnie did that once in a while. So caught up in the magic of the season, she'd forget to turn them off during the day. Grief seized his chest. Losing her during the holidays... That made it so much worse.

He tried to shake it off as he returned to his seat. "Did you remember that heavy duty extension cord?"

Shane kicked a nearby box. "Right here."

"Thanks. I need to head over there and finish the Christmas display. I don't know what the B&B will look like next year, but this year that place will look like Winnie always made it look for Christmas."

"That's the spirit. Need any help?"

"Nah, I got it."

Shane tapped at his keyboard. "Before you go, check out this e-mail I'm forwarding. We have more work."

Cole studied his screen. "Really? We got a security contract for the school district? You buried the lead, my friend. I can't believe you didn't text me when this came in."

"I was confirming the details."

"I thought this kind of thing was settled at the start of the school year."

"It's settled with the budget year but I think there were some issues and the school board got all hot about something and voided an agreement by way of a loophole."

"Works for me."

"Small town politics. Plus, it's a small district. All we had to do was come in lower than the hourly rate of the off-duty Cardinal Point PD."

"This cuts into their overtime revenue. Might cost us some friends and allies."

"Business, Cole. They'll have a chance to outbid us another time."

Yeah, that was enough to raise a spike of anger in Cole's gut. He was a trained military police officer with more hours, more training, and more experience than anyone on that force. But instead of working for them, he had to make a living as a glorified mall cop because of his hearing loss. He let out a deep sigh. No matter. He and Shane were going to expand their services. From basic security to self-defense classes and specialized surveillance, they'd make it work.

"That's not the best part," Shane said, "read on."

"Seriously? The high school principal from the home of the Mighty Fighting Redbirds has requested armed security for the annual Snowball Dance?"

Shane laughed. "Yup."

"Why? I'm pretty sure we'd get by with a reflective vest and the big flashlight. Why does he want armed security?"

"Deterrent. That's all. Teenagers in a growing community. Keep 'em in line."

"Whatever. It's a paycheck." He slid his keys in his pocket. "I'm headin' over to Winnie's to get those lights up. Cold snap coming tomorrow, too. I need to make sure the house is ready..." His thought trailed off into a sad haze. Winnie's house. Chilled and empty. There was something completely wrong about that and it could never be made right again.

"You OK, buddy?"

"Yeah. I can't believe she's not there."

Shane nodded. "Wait up, I'll come with you."

"Nah, really. It's fine. You've got the door at bingo tonight, right?"

"Yup."

"Text me if you need me."

"I will. And Cole," Shane said as he raised his cup, "here's to Winnie. One of the finest women we'll ever know." He took a swig. "And to the mysterious niece. May she be smokin' hot, single, and a lot like her Aunt Winnie."

Cole cracked his first real smile in three days. "Hear, hear."

ੴ

The generic female voice of the GPS system scraped the last layer of flesh from the back of Jacey's neck. She'd traveled five states and over a thousand miles with this woman and, like a bad roommate, it was time to go their separate ways. Luckily, she should be pulling up to her destination at any time.

From a national title winning collegiate gymnastics coach to a B&B owner... how weird was that? Weirder still, discovering a maternal aunt she never knew existed. She scarcely remembered her mother, let alone other family.

A large wooden sign with a Cardinal in the corner announced the Cardinal Point Bed and Breakfast. She turned into the tree-lined lane and made her way up a gravel drive. A two-story snow-white Victorian with jet black shutters came into view. Half of the house was simply adorable. The other half looked like Santa's workshop threw up on it.

It was covered, top to bottom, with holiday decorations. There was tinsel, garland, and inflatables. Wooden cut-outs in colorful cellophane, wrapped to look like lollipops, dotted the yard. Christmas lights were strung, draped, and twirled around anything that didn't move.

Scratch that. The train running atop the porch rail had lights attached to it.

But the absolute show stopper in this redneck pageant of Yule excess was the giant plastic manger, complete with Mary, Joseph, and the baby

Jesus, being prayed over by a kneeling Santa. Out of respect, Santa had removed his cowboy hat.

Someone, shoot me now.

At best, she was a bit of a Scrooge. At worst, she made the Grinch look like a holiday party planner. Had she mentioned she was homeless, broke and unemployed? Definitely a worst kind of year. And why was only half of the house decorated?

She parked in a gravel lot next to the Noel side of the house. Moe was glued to the window. "It's a lot to take in, isn't it, pooch?"

After she clipped the leash onto the dog's collar, they made their way up the walk. Music blared from a docking station on the undecorated side of the wraparound porch. As she rounded the corner, a man wearing faded jeans and a gray sweatshirt stood with his back to her. Head bent, it appeared he was untangling an orange extension cord as a cool December breeze whipped through his black hair.

"Hello. I'm Jacey Steele."

No reaction.

She took a few cautious steps forward and slipped her hand into her purse to find her pepper spray. She didn't take it out, but she had her finger securely on the trigger, just in case. He was a stranger, after all.

"Sir? Hello." She raised her voice to be heard above the music. "Who are you?"

Still no response.

She inched closer, fingers tightening on the pepper spray. Moe yipped and yanked on his leash, anxious to greet a new friend. "Hey! Sir, can you hear me? I'm Jacey Steele, the new owner."

Nothing.

This was ridiculous. She marched up and tapped him on the shoulder. "Hey, buddy, I'm talking to you."

He jerked around. "I'm sorry, what?"

Dramatic deep green eyes nearly knocked her off her rant—that and his striking good looks.

Yum.

And she rarely did yum. Who had time for yum?

He opened his mouth again. "Can I help you?"

She remembered why she was ranting in the first place. "I've been trying to get your attention for five minutes. Are you deaf?"

"As a matter of fact, yes."

"I'm Jac—wait. What?"

He dropped the extension cord and stepped over to turn off the music. "I. Am. Deaf. Or mostly deaf."

Sure her cheeks were as red as Rudolph's nose, she stepped back and placed her palm against her forehead. "This is an all-time social low. Rock bottom on the politeness scale. First, I bully my well-intentioned lawyer, now I've insulted the disabled. Maybe later I can drive by the pre-school and tell everyone there's no Santa." And now she was aware that while he probably couldn't hear her, he could most definitely *see* her rambling like a maniac. "I'm… ah… I'm so sorry."

He shoved his hands into the front pocket of his hoodie. "Are you sorry because I'm deaf?" One side of his mouth kicked up. "Or because you're rude?"

Was he teasing her?

She blew hair from her eyes and met his grass green gaze. "Both, I guess. Hey, are you reading my lips?" She leaned in. "You are. What'd I just say?"

The half-smile morphed into a rakish grin. "Apology accepted for the rudeness. You didn't have anything to do with me being deaf. That honor goes to an IED in Afghanistan. I'm Cole Boudreaux. And, yes, I read lips."

He extended his hand.

Rather than take it, she continued to stare. "Are you Mr. Boudreaux's son?"

"Yes. You knew my father?"

"Knew? Is he uh… dead?" She wasn't proud of the little thought skittering through her head. If Mr. Boudreaux had died, wouldn't she be the sole owner of the B&B? Inappropriate, she knew—but desperate times and all.

"Yes, for seven years."

"Virgil Coleman Boudreaux has been dead for seven years?"

"Yes and no." His mouth inched up on one side again.

"I'm sorry. I have no idea what you're talking about."

"My father was Virgil Coleman Boudreaux, Jr. He is dead. My grandpa, on the other hand, is the original Virgil Coleman Boudreaux and he is very much alive. I am Virgil Coleman Boudreaux the third. I am not dead," he said flatly. Then his extremely nice mouth spread into an extremely nice smile. "I go by Cole, for obvious reasons."

"Fascinating… So where can I find the original Mr. Boudreaux?"

"Grandpa? This time of day he's probably at the house watching *Jeopardy*." Cole frowned and scratched the side of his head. "He didn't find you on the Internet, did he? I told him that was a bad idea."

"Excuse me?"

"I told him there were plenty of nice ladies his age at the rec center, but OK." He glanced at the ground and followed the bright orange cord to its end. "I can give you the address if you really want to go through with this thing."

"What... *thing*?"

He shot her a wicked grin over his shoulder. "I'm kidding." After a long, uncomfortable pause he turned to her. "It was a joke."

Jacey stepped back and crossed her arms. "I can see you're enjoying your little uh... whatever this is, but I am the new owner of this B&B and I have business to attend to, so if you would please tell me where to find Mr. Boudreaux..."

The man stopped and straightened. The muscles moved across his back as he took a deep breath and turned to face her.

"You're Jacey, Winnie's niece."

"Winnie, of course. I've only seen her name as Winifred."

"I'm the Cole Boudreaux you're looking for. I guess we have a lot to talk about. Come on in. I'll make coffee." He disappeared into the house.

She hiked her purse higher on her shoulder. "I guess we're going inside, Moe."

As soon as they entered her aunt's home, she unclipped Moe's leash. He took off after Cole, leaving Jacey alone in the entrance hall.

If the outside of the house was overdone, the inside was downright... Well, if there were décor police, Aunt Winnie would have died in prison.

Two steps over the threshold and it was attack of the clichés. There were catchy sayings all over the place. Inspirational platitudes were printed, painted and woven into rugs, pillows, plaques, dishes, mirrors, and even rocks.

When God closes a door, he opens a window.

God is good all the time, and all the time God is good.

Jesus is the reason for the season.

Happiness is a choice.

Let go, and let God.

I can do all things through Christ who strengthens me.

And the ever popular, *Jesus Take the Wheel*.

The entire space was engraved, scrolled and calligraphied to within an inch of its life with scripture and Christian drivel.

And she was only in the foyer.

So her aunt was a holy roller? Interesting. Could that explain why they'd never met? Her father had no tolerance for religious *mumbo-jumbo*, as he called it. Frankly, she didn't have any use for it, either.

There were gymnasts who prayed before meets and they still lost. Or, they told her they'd pray for her and she'd fall on beam anyway. One of the few times she was allowed to spend the night with a friend, she'd gone to church with the girl's family. At first, it was fine. The people were nice and she liked the singing, but when the guy started preaching about sin and hell, she felt horrible about herself. She wasn't ever good enough at home, so she didn't need to go to church and get the same treatment.

Scoring in the top three isn't good enough, Jacey. When you win the All-Around, then you'll have accomplished something.

If God was all about sin and never measuring up, she had her own version of a living, breathing god at home, and he was called Dad. She'd had a lifetime of working herself to death to win multiple All-Arounds, and he still demanded her to be better.

So she'd worked and won the All-Around again and again, but it was never good enough.

Where was God when she was having the life sucked out of her?

And why did God take the good parent and leave her with the tyrant?

She followed the clink of mugs to the kitchen, where she found Cole pouring two cups of coffee. He placed a bowl of water on the floor for Moe. The dog showed his appreciation by yipping, licking, and finally rolling over on his back while Cole rubbed his belly.

Come on, Moe, have a little pride.

He surveyed the kitchen and gave her a sad smile. "I can't believe she's gone."

"I'm sorry for your loss."

He tunneled his fingers through his short black hair. "I'm sorry for you, too."

"Why?" Her insides constricted. What did he know?

"For the loss of your aunt." He said each word slowly like she was the one who was deaf.

"Oh." She nudged the Frosty the Snowman salt and pepper shaker. "Thanks, but I didn't know her." She gave Frosty another poke as Cole's nice mouth flat lined.

"She was a wonderful person. Kind, generous, and she loved Jesus more than any other person I've ever known."

She gave him a smile she hoped appeared genuine and scanned the hutch full of recipe books. The décor was the same country kitsch as the foyer. With glass green walls and purple and yellow accents, the homey space was inviting. Besides all the religious stuff, the rest of the kitchen spoke to a forgotten place inside her and made her feel at home. At least the lawsuit and mounting bills seemed far, far away. She took a deep drag of air into her lungs. It was the first good breath she'd taken in days, weeks, maybe ever.

Cole placed a cup of coffee in her hand.

"Are there any guests here, or is the house empty?" She perused the jam-packed walls and added, "Of people?"

"Empty. The inn was booked for the month of December, but I sent cancellation emails. Everyone had really nice things to say about Winnie."

She nodded. It was clear this guy was torn up over her aunt's death, but she had no idea what to do or say.

He rummaged in a drawer and pulled out an old address book. "I haven't heard back from the McKillips, but they live in an RV year round so they might not have seen their email. I'll look again for a number."

"When were they supposed to arrive?"

"Monday. I'm sure we'll hear from them before then."

She set her mug next to Frosty and planted her hands on her hips. "This is going to be a lot of work."

"Yep. It is. But I'll help as much as I can."

"Thanks. Do you know where we can get some boxes?"

He tilted his head to the side. "For what?"

Her hand swept out in front of her like one of the women on *The Price is Right*. "To pack away the majority of this stuff."

"What? Why?"

"Realtors hate clutter."

"A realtor? For what?"

"I'm selling the B&B."

TWO

Cole tapped dirt off the edge of his boot and made his way to the kitchen door at Winnie's B&B. The cold leather of his jacket squeaked as he maneuvered a tray of coffee and a bag of muffins in his hands. The weatherman's prediction was more accurate than usual. The temperature had dropped and dusted central Texas with its first layer of frost. The scent of winter settled around him and mingled with the cinnamon pinecone branch hanging on a nearby hook. For a split second he just knew Winnie was waiting inside.

She was not.

And that was too sad to think about when the long-lost niece was probably there instead, taking inventory and assembling boxes to cart Winnie's life to a storage shed.

He shouldered open the screen door and grabbed the brass knob. He stopped. While he hadn't knocked on Winnie's kitchen door, well... ever, he probably should start since a stranger lived there now. At least temporarily.

In hindsight, he maybe should've called, too, but Jacey Steele seemed determined to keep moving.

Shoulders back and spine straight, the petite, honey-blonde beauty had stepped through the house with more curiosity than sorrow or even warmth. She clearly didn't know her Aunt Winnie, and the B&B was nothing more to her than an inconvenience. So he would try to keep up with the seemingly high-strung dynamo who carried the chill into town on the sparkle of her crisp blue eyes.

Moe pranced and pawed at the door as it opened. He gave Cole a sloppy greeting before he charged for the nearest clump of bushes.

"Cole," Jacey said. "I wasn't expecting you."

"Yeah. Sorry about that." He left the door cracked for Moe and set everything on the table. If hummingbird muffins and coffee from Songbird's Bakery and Café didn't soften her up, nothing would. "I brought breakfast."

She tucked a piece of hair behind her ear and peeked in the bag. "Carbs."

"Aw, man, sorry." He draped his coat on a chair and sat down. "Are you strictly no sugar?"

She fumbled with the stirrer she'd taken from the cardboard tray. Pink hit her cheeks like a splash of watermelon and then she paled. "Wait. That was rude. Thank you. They smell great."

"They are great. Songbird's is the best and only bakery in town. There's one in the grocery store, but nobody believes they make their own muffins."

Really, Cole? No one believes they make their own muffins? Lame...

"I'm not strictly 'no sugar'." She closed the door on Moe's return and joined him at the table. "But I do eat healthy. My job demands it."

Now they were getting somewhere. He hadn't missed her fit body, especially since it was covered in a black and green version of the workout gear he saw on women at the gym. "Are you a trainer or a nutritionist or something?"

"Gymnastics coach. Florida Northern College."

"That's impressive. So you're on Christmas break?"

"Something like that."

"You drove all the way from Florida?"

She pinched off a piece of muffin. "Yep. Just me and Moe."

The dog's ears pricked at the sound of his name, but he never stopped his eyes-deep plunge into his food bowl.

"How did you sleep? Do you like the Isaac & Rebekah room?"

Her nose twitched like she was trying to manage a smile but couldn't quite get her mouth to cooperate.

"It's nice," she said. "A little cold and a little weird to be here alone. I'm not familiar with all the usual creaks."

"It's an old house. It makes a lot of noise. Winnie was updating one thing at a time, but it's a big job. We were going to tackle the upstairs windows in the spring." He stopped when he remembered their discussion about how double-paned glass would be more efficient. She was there counting windows one day and gone the next. "There are extra quilts and blankets everywhere," he added in a rush to move on.

"Thank you. I'll find them."

"And, if you're still uncomfortable, you can move to the Abraham & Sarah room. It gets the afternoon sun."

She nodded.

Cole crumpled an empty sugar packet into his palm. "And you uh... You had no idea you had an aunt here in Texas?"

She shook her head. "I've been wracking my brain. I see her things and her pictures and I smell this kitchen and I think I'm right on the edge of some memory, but nothing comes clear."

"She was your mother's sister, right?"

"Yes."

"'Cause I've been thinking, too. I seem to remember she mentioned a sister who died, but she wouldn't say much about it. I was here all the time but I didn't get into her personal things. If there are pictures or documents, I haven't seen them." He tossed the sugar packet on the table. "If you don't mind my asking, is your dad still alive?"

"Yes."

"And he doesn't know anything?"

"We haven't really talked about it and we..." She grabbed a stack of clean napkins and unfolded and refolded the first two. "It doesn't matter. We haven't talked about it."

And with that, Cole could tell she meant they hadn't talked at all but didn't want to admit it. Whatever her family drama, the little gymnast from the Sunshine State was holding tight to some personal issues and he guessed they weren't pretty. It was day two of the mysterious niece and he hadn't seen her smile a real smile once.

"Tell you what," he said and stood. "Grab a jacket and get Moe's leash. You didn't know Winnie, and frankly, it's too late for that and a darn shame. But you can get to know the town she loved."

"There's no time," she said and gathered their trash. "I have to make some calls. We need to talk about this place. We have decisions to make."

"So we'll walk and talk."

"The refrigerator." She pointed at it as if to protest. "It has a bad smell. I need to get in there and see what that's about."

Cole froze with one arm in his coat. Of course. Winnie shopped. And cooked. And after the funeral, her friends came with food. Leftovers and sour milk hadn't crossed his mind. What else had he forgotten? What else did he need to do?

He slipped his other arm in and pulled the zipper halfway. "Look, Jacey, I'll be honest with you. I get that you had no idea about Winnie or this place and I get that you want to sell. You're her real family so I won't stand in your way. But it's different for me and the people around here. It's been a bad couple of weeks. And just so you know, I can't afford to buy you out or I would, and I won't let you buy me out because it's not about that for me. So grab a jacket and get Moe's leash and let's take a walk into town."

As long, awkward pauses went, it was worse than most.

"Sure," she finally said on a whisper. "I'll meet you outside."

಄಄

Cole always wanted a dog. Probably a German Shepherd or a Doberman. A big dog with personality and discipline. A dog that would run with him in the mornings, guard the house while he was away, and curl up at night for a good scratch in front of the TV. A well-trained dog with good manners.

Moe was not that dog.

The little mutt was sweet enough, but did hard-as-nails Coach Jacey Steele just pick him up because she thought the sidewalk was too cold for his feet? What a sissy-dog.

"It warms up around here pretty fast," he said.

She answered him as they left the side street and turned onto the main drag to the square, but he didn't catch it. He had rules to help him hear. Put the phone to his 'good' ear. Keep people to his right when walking or sitting in restaurants. Look straight at baristas, bank tellers and clients, and observe every movement for body language clues. Forget drive-thrus. People with normal hearing couldn't always catch what came out of a static-filled speaker. Why torture himself?

Then there was Jacey and that sissy-dog. She finally set him down, only to have him strain at his leash and pull her down the street and back and forth across the walk. He sniffed, licked and violated everything that couldn't get away. Cole had imagined more of a stroll through Winnie's stomping ground, accompanied by stimulating and informative conversation. Jacey clearly had more of a foot-race-slash-tug-of-war in mind. Not with him, but with her dog.

Conclusion: These two didn't know how to take a proper walk.

He stopped by the big stone planter outside The Perfect Purl yarn and fabric store. "Hold up, Jacey."

She strode back, and Moe hiked his leg on the planter. For the second time.

"Yes?"

"I was hoping we could walk together. And talk. And look at some of the downtown."

She seemed surprised. "We are walking and talking and seeing things."

"Fine. Don't turn around. What is the name of this store we're standing right in front of?"

She scrunched her lightly freckled nose and looked to the sky. She moved.

"I said don't turn around."

"All right, ya got me. I don't know."

"This is The Perfect Purl. They do all things thread and fabric and crafty sewing stuff. Maddie and her partner Isabel were friends of Winnie's. They tried to teach her to knit for five years. It didn't take, and frustrated Winnie to no end. In fact, Winnie's needles are buried in her herb garden. Maddie and Isabel think she lost them. Now. How is that not an entertaining story?"

Jacey turned and shielded her eyes from the bright morning sun to study the storefront. "You're right," she said as she turned back. "I'm sorry. It's a great story."

"This is the best time of day to be here. Stores are opening for business. All the tourists haven't converged on the square yet."

"So it gets a lot of visitors?"

"Yeah. As you can see, the B&B is only 3 blocks from this part of town. That's why it's always full. People love to shop this small town charm year around. The big retailers are starting to move in, but they're out near the freeway."

She nodded.

"You probably came right through here when you got to town."

She scanned the decorated streets. "Yes. I remember a toy store on the corner."

"Yep. Ella's Creative Play. It also has a children's reading room."

"Is there a story about that, too?"

"There might be."

She had the beginnings of what might have been a smile, but she turned and charged ahead before he could see it or clearly hear what she said as she walked away.

He stood firm. "Jacey, come back."

Moe made a loop and fell over on his side near her feet. "What now?"

"I have a seventy-five percent hearing loss in my left ear, and a fifty percent loss in my right. With the street noise and the wind, I can't always hear you when you're walking and talking way ahead of me. Would it be possible for you to slow down and walk and talk *with* me?"

"Once again, I apologize, but I thought that's what we were doing."

"Give me the leash."

"Why? I'm walking my dog."

"No, what you're doing resembles flying a kite. That dog is all over the place and you're chasing him like he's in charge. Where do you walk him in

Florida? An airport runway or something? He can't even stay on the sidewalk and it's about to get busy out here."

Yep. Another record-breaking pregnant pause.

"Hey, look, I'm sorry," he said. "Not my place to tell you how to walk your dog. Florida's real nice and all and you probably take some great scenic walks. Moe's probably confused with all the Victorian Christmas vibe around here. Are you close enough to jog on the beach?"

She scuffed her cross-trainer along the ground. "There are some large grassy areas on campus. He plays there." She handed over the leash. "Here, you take him."

He'd asked for it, but was still surprised when she turned it over. "OK."

He took off, Moe fell in line with his stride, and the cute little gymnast shoved her hands in her pockets and walked beside him. He couldn't be sure, but he thought maybe he just taught a fierce twenty-something college coach how to take a walk.

For an entire block, she said next to nothing. It wasn't his ears. He wasn't missing a thing. He'd pointed out a couple places of interest, and she had nothing to say.

He stopped at the light. Moe paused as if proud of himself and waited for the go-ahead. Jacey chewed on her lip, eyes front.

"You really don't like small talk, do you?"

She shook her head and glanced at the curb as if embarrassed. "Honestly, I don't talk to a lot of people. It's my job to talk *at* them. To direct and instruct. I give a lot of orders."

He smiled wide. That sounded familiar. "You and I aren't that different, you know." He motioned for them to cross. "I told you I'm military. Give orders, take orders. The circle of life."

"How long have you been home?"

"A little more than a year."

"Have you and Winnie been running the B&B together for a long time?"

"No, not at all. That was Winnie's baby. We've been friends for years. I helped her out and she was like a mother to me, but no... I was totally shocked when she left half of it to me."

"Oh. Then what do you do?"

"My friend and I own a security company."

Back to silence.

Most days he hated the quiet and welcomed conversation so he could remember he still heard things besides the incessant ringing inside his head. But if a woman doesn't want to talk to you, she doesn't want to talk. He didn't usually have that problem. Most women wanted to gab what was left of his ears off. Then again, there was the one woman who never wanted to speak with him again.

Annalise.

Broke his heart, that one did. When he was deployed, they were planning a wedding. When he returned, there was nothing. Annalise didn't want damaged goods. She'd shut him up, shut him out, and shut him down. Engagement over.

Beside him, Jacey seemed to have taken great interest in the side of his head. She stepped around a giant nutcracker outside the candy store and continued to stare. She slowed.

"Do you have a hearing aide in there?"

"In where, exactly?"

She stopped. Her eyes got as big as one of Winnie's cake plates.

He laughed because it was funny.

"You're laughing at me."

"No," he said and laughed again. "I thought I was being funny, but apparently I wasn't."

"I shouldn't have asked a personal question," she said and stomped forward.

"Jacey, wait. It's not a big deal. C'mon, we were doing so well with the walking thing."

She dropped to a bench near a yaupon tree covered with twinkle lights. Moe hopped up beside her. Cole sat to her left and stretched his arm across the back.

"I don't get out of the gym much," she said. "There's not a lot of time to socialize in my world. I think it's safe to say I'm not very good at it."

"No worries. Sounds intense. Competitive gymnastics must be an all-or-nothing kind of sport. You're not the first person dedicated to that lifestyle. Gotta make a living."

"You have no idea…"

She paused. Intensity settled on her face as if she contemplated every possible phrase that could next come out of her mouth. What was so heavy on her mind that a simple conversation proved too difficult?

"My father," she continued, "was all business, discipline, and focus when it came to my gymnastics. He didn't allow any outside distractions. It was an isolated existence. Everything was directed toward the mat or the beam… even my grief had to make way for training." She stopped the stream of information as if stemming the flow of an open, bleeding wound. "Anyway, that's why I didn't know my Aunt Winnie, I'm sure. I wasn't allowed anything but the journey to the top."

Well, that would explain her lack of communication skills.

Everything he wanted to say would come out as pity, and he had a feeling she didn't want anyone to feel sorry for her. But how could he help it? He did pity her and her closed world. He didn't care much for her father, either, and he didn't even know the guy.

"That's rough, Jacey," he finally managed to say. "I can only believe Winnie would have made your life better. I know she made mine better." Boy, did she. "I lost my parents when I was younger, too, and was a disaster when I got returned from active duty. Winnie allowed me one week to wallow in the loss of my hearing and some other stuff. Then she knocked me into shape with the love of Jesus and a swift kick. Only Winnie knew how to do all that with a *Bless Your Heart* still on her lips."

"Yeah, well, a lot of things would have been different if a lot of things would've been different. Can't change it now."

"I don't have aides, by the way. It's in the works. I got sidetracked with my business and some other things this past year. The VA's moving slow on my case, too."

"Do your doctors think it will help?"

"Can't see as it will hurt." He stood and tugged Moe's leash. "C'mon. One more stop then we'll head back."

"Where?"

"The toy store's right here on the corner. You mentioned it so I thought you might want to go in. I'll introduce you to Ella—another good friend of Winnie's."

"No, I uh… I don't need to go in."

But even as she protested, she headed for the window and practically pressed her nose to it.

"Are you sure you don't want to go in?"

"I'm sure."

"Do you see one you need for your collection or something?"

"No. I don't collect dolls. Tyrant father, remember?"

"Yeah. Sorry. Every woman I know has some kind of collection. Unicorns, bunnies… Gwendolyn on the other corner collects hair. Makes jewelry out of it. Totally creepy."

Now she just looked annoyed. "I don't collect anything, but if you really want to help me, you could tell me if there's a gym where I can work out while I'm here. We also need a good realtor."

"Sure." He worked Moe's leash between his fingers. "My grandpa uses Chip Bentley. I'll call him and tell him to come by the B&B. As for working out, go to the rec center. Tell them who you are and that I sent you. They'll give you a visitor pass for however long you need it."

She nodded. "I need to get back."

"Whatever you say."

Jacey took one last look in the window. Something all Christmassy and hopeful crossed her face.

Poof!

It was gone.

CR&O

Gloria Gaynor may survive the storms of life, but Jacey wasn't so sure she would. She yanked out her earbuds and powered down the treadmill. Things were bad if *I Will Survive*, her favorite girl power song, couldn't motivate her.

The Cardinal Point rec center was impressively furnished with free-weights, machines and an assortment of cardio equipment. She loved to exercise. Too bad she couldn't get out of her own head long enough to enjoy all this place had to offer.

As she stretched her hamstrings, the events of the last couple of days filtered through her head. Cole's charismatic green gaze, quirky sense of humor, and unexpected kindness wrapped around her like a well-loved quilt. Even so, it made her look for the closest exit, and run for the hills. Sweat slid down her cheeks and pooled in the hollow of her throat. She swiped at it with a pink embroidered towel she found at Winnie's. And if her conflicted, convoluted feelings about a deaf soldier weren't enough, a disturbing volcano of resentment threatened to spew when she considered the loving woman whose home burst at the seams with moralistic platitudes.

If Winnie was such a fine Christian and so very caring, why did she wait until she died to reach out to her only family member? Why hadn't Winnie ever come to look for her? Old feelings of not being good enough or lovable enough made her achy and tight, like her muscles were folding in on themselves. A good stretch would help.

She placed her hand against the treadmill's handle, bent her knee, and grabbed her ankle to stretch her quads. The lonely little girl that lived just beneath the surface of her skin sobbed for never knowing a relative with so much love to give. But the grown woman practically vibrated with contempt for such a hypocrite as her Aunt Winnie.

So what? Life wasn't fair. If she'd learned anything in her twenty-something years it was that definite little nugget of truth.

After Jacey finished her stretch, she gathered her workout bag and made her way to the front of the rec center. Squeals and laughter came from inside the gymnasium across from the fitness room.

When she paused to dig for her keys, a sudden movement caught her eye. "Stop!" She dropped her bag and charged into the gym in time to pluck a little red-haired girl out of mid-air and set her firmly onto her feet. "Who's in charge here?" She scanned the stunned expressions of the little gymnasts assembled before her.

Well, nine were stunned. One was enraged.

"Hey. I was doing a back handspring and you messed me up." Small fists slammed on her black and yellow leotard-clad hips. She looked like a ticked-off bumblebee.

"No, I didn't mess you up, but I might have saved your life. There's no way you were making past your neck. Where is your coach?"

There wasn't a single adult around.

A tiny blond in a blue polka-dot bathing suit that doubled as a leotard, raised her hand. "Miss Tammy went to the bathroom. She told us not to get on the equipment or tumble until she got back." She shot the bumblebee a closed-lip smile.

Bumblebee stuck her tongue out at Blondie.

"Stop that." Jacey stepped between the two. "Where's the bathroom?"

A loud thud jerked her attention to the far end of the gym. A round woman in a Christmas top, black leggings, and tan knock-off ankle boots came coasting into the gym. Her big baby bump was swathed in Rudolph's face, complete with a red pom-pom nose in the dead center of the bulge. "I swear this baby is camping on my bladder. All right, girls line up. Oh. Who are you?" She tilted her head. Auburn cork-screw curls bounced like swirly Christmas ribbon.

Jacey prepared to blast the woman. Disregard for safety pushed all of her hot buttons, since a totally preventable injury ended her Olympic dream and gymnastics career. "I'm Jacey Steele, I'm new in town."

"Hello, I'm Tammy Patty." Her pudgy little hand flew to her cheek. "Oh, my word, your Winnie's niece." Suddenly, Jacey was smothered by arms, baby, reindeer, and bouncy curls. Tammy hugged her tight. "Your aunt was so awesome. We all loved her very much." She released her death grip and glanced from Jacey to the girls. Her brow furrowed into little groves of concentration as if she were trying to fit the pieces together. When she tilted her head, her jingle bell earrings clinked. "What are you doing here?"

She pointed at the bee. "I happened to walk by and see this girl attempting a back handspring without proper technique or a spotter. If I hadn't intervened, you'd be facing an injury lawsuit."

Tammy's lip began to quiver.

"No need to cry. I handled it. No harm, no foul. It's all good, see?" She grabbed the bumblebee and put her between the gestating woman and herself.

Tammy blinked furiously and finally seemed to master her emotions. She wrapped her arms around her belly. "Oh my cheese and crackers. Thank you, Jesus. Kari, didn't I specifically tell y'all not to tumble or get on the equipment while I was in the bathroom?"

Bumblebee stared at the ground. "Yes, ma'am."

Tammy placed a finger under the girls chin and raised it to look her into her eyes. "What do you have to say to me?"

"I'm sorry, Miss Tammy."

Jacey was appalled when Tammy wrapped the child in a hug and told her to go stand with the others. The little rule breaker wasn't being punished? "That's it? That's all you're going to do? She could've been seriously injured and needs to be taught a lesson."

"You're absolutely right, Jacey. Kari, come here." The offender stood in front of them. "Darlin'," Tammy said, "the reason I asked you to stay off of the equipment and not to tumble is because you could be badly hurt. And wouldn't it be a shame if you got injured and couldn't march in the annual Christmas parade? Now, I hope you've learned your lesson."

Big crocodile tears shimmered in Kari's eyes. "Yes, ma'am."

"It's time to go, everyone." She beamed a smile at the girls. "Good work today."

They all scattered like birdseed on the wind. Jacey shook her head. As reprimands went, that one stunk.

"Thank you for your concern and for the helpful advice to make sure Kari learned her lesson. Maribeth!" Jacey nearly jumped out of her skin when Tammy screamed. "Let go of Beth Anne's hair or I will make you two hug for ten minutes! Y'all go get your baby sister from the toddler room."

"You have three children, you're pregnant, and you coach? How do you have the time?"

Tammy blew a curl from her eyes. "Yes, the twins are mine and on the team, plus I have a nineteen month old in childcare. But I'm not the actual coach. Coach Haley moved six weeks ago. I was a gymnast in middle school and since part of team belongs to me, I volunteered to help until a new coach could be hired."

"What level gymnast were you?" Jacey was distracted by something on Tammy's shirt that peeked out every time her hair swayed. Was it more Christmas decoration? She honestly didn't know how the woman could fit one more festive thing on the garment.

"Level? Oh, no. I did recreational gymnastics." Tammy giggled. "I wasn't on a team."

One of Tammy's twins jogged up with a toddler in her arms. The little girl leaned out of her sister's arms for her mother to hold her. Tammy took the child and plopped her on one hip. Jacey barely noticed the child as she still couldn't figure out what was hiding beneath Tammy's hair.

"How do you—is that a Froot Loop on your shirt?"

Tammy flipped a curl out of the way and plucked the little pink ring from her top. "Huh. Well, look at that."

Jacey watched in horror as Tammy handed the cereal to the baby who popped it into her mouth. The germ-a-phobe in Jacey fought the urge to perform the Heimlich on the slobbery child. No way could that be healthy. And why were they both laughing like idiots? "Ah… It was nice to meet you Tammy, but I need to be going."

"All right, don't be a stranger." Her clueless, yet contagious smile spread like sunshine.

Jacey turned to escape at the same time Cole strolled up and draped his arm around Tammy. "What are you ladies so happy about?" He kissed the top of her head. "Woman, if you get any more beautiful, I might have to steal you away from that cousin of mine."

Where had he come from? Jacey supposed she should expect stealth from a former solider.

"Oh, Cole, you big ol' flirt." Rudolph's nose jiggled as Tammy snickered.

"I see you met Jacey. I hope you were nice to her." He rubbed his big hand over the baby's tow-head.

Tammy slapped his arm. "You know I was nice. When have you ever known me not to be nice?"

Jacey observed the bi-play between Cole and Tammy, fascinated. One wore her breakfast on her shirt and probably carried an extra thirty pounds, the other was near deaf, but both seemed perfectly comfortable with themselves and each other.

In her world, perfection was all that mattered. People strove for it, fought for it, and some nearly killed themselves for it. She'd lived her whole life on that hamster wheel and it hadn't bought her one ounce of happiness.

At least not as much joy as a found Froot Loop shoved in a baby's mouth.

THREE

Jacey lugged boxes into Winnie's study. On her way home from the rec center, she'd mentally reviewed her list of things to do, and decided the roll-top desk was as good a place as any to find important papers and start *Operation Declutter*.

Unease crawled up her vertebrae. She had every right to comb through the contents of her estranged aunt's home. In theory, that was true, but a discomfort continued to dog her.

Calm down, Jacey, it's just a desk.

Dread slung a beefy arm over her shoulder. At some point, she would have to go through Winnie's clothes and personal items. Maybe Cole knew some of Winnie's friends who would help with that task. Yes. That would work.

Problem solved.

Her apprehension eased a bit when Moe sauntered into the room. The click of his nails on the hardwood floor gave her a sense of familiarity in the unfamiliar house.

"Hey, Moe-Moe. Do you want to help?"

The dog turned three circles, plopped in front of an overstuffed floral chair next to a small basket, and tucked his nose under his paws.

"Guess not."

A vague sense of déjà vu tugged at her as she saw the basket full of toys. Like a fish playing with a baited hook, a dim memory tugged at her then quickly fled. Had she played in this room before? No. She'd never been to Winnie's. Still, she couldn't shake the creepy feeling.

There was a radio in the window behind Winnie's desk, circa 1980. She flipped it on, and Christmas carols filled the room. The music made her think of Tammy's jingly sweatshirt and her band of renegade gymnasts. They looked adorable in their little leotards. The mother of three-and-a-half definitely had her hands full with that group.

Stop stalling, Steele, and get to work.

For the next half hour, she sorted through bills to determine the ones that needed to be paid immediately. Thankfully, it didn't appear Winnie kept her finances like she kept her house. Everything was organized and orderly. She even had online bill pay for the essentials. A tsunami of relief rolled over her when the bank statements indicated there was enough money in Winnie's account to pay the bills. She certainly didn't have the funds to take care of them.

As she surfed through the accounts, she wondered how Winnie became so tech savvy. Had Cole helped her? He seemed ready to do what needed to be done. A warm candle glow kindled in her chest when she thought of Cole. He'd been nothing but kind since she'd arrived and she was sure she'd been nothing but a burr under his saddle.

She shook off thoughts of the handsome soldier and moved to the other contents of the desk. She labeled three piles—*keep*, *toss*, and *check with Cole*. The next time she looked at her watch an hour had gone by and the box of garbage was nearly full. Moe came over and nudged her leg with his nose. "Aw, Moe, have I been ignoring you?" She picked up the pooch and nuzzled his fur. "I have one more drawer to go through, and then we'll find some food." He licked her face, jumped down, and trotted back to his spot next to the chair.

The bottom drawer was the largest and contained labeled organizers. The first file held reservation information for the B&B. The next one, warranties for the air conditioner, hot water heater, and other household appliances. She made a note to have Cole to go through the contents of that folder. In all, there were ten categories. She'd been through nine and there'd been nothing too exciting in any of them.

"Last one, Moe. Then we eat." Good thing, too, because she could feel her back tightening. She'd been sitting too long.

When she removed the last file marked *Personal*, a stack of letters tied together with a black ribbon fell to the floor. Pain bit into her spine like barbed wire when she leaned over to pick them up. "Ouch. I have the body of a ninety-year-old woman, Moe."

Thank you, gymnastics.

She tossed the bundle onto the desk and stood to stretch her hamstrings and lower back. When she rose, her name on the top envelope caught her eye. She quickly thumbed through the stack and saw they were all addressed to her, and they all had *Return to Sender* stamped across the front. Her heart bucked like a wild Mustang.

What? How? Why?

The three words chased each other around her head. The first letter appeared in her hand and was open before she had time to think better of it. Silver glitter fell to the desk when she withdrew a birthday card with four scoops of ice cream in a cone on the front. Under the cone it read *Four scoops of sweetness... For the sweetest FOUR-year-old around!* Inside, a note read:

Jacey,

I hope you have the most wonderful, amazing, spectacular, stupendous birthday and that it's filled with love, happiness, and truckloads of ice cream!

I love and miss you every day. I pray God's hand of protection is on you forever.

All my love,

Aunt Winnie

Like a starving child, she ripped into each envelope and devoured the contents. The letters spanned years. There were birthday, Christmas, and Valentine's Day greetings. Each indicated there was a corresponding gift to go with the card.

She'd never received any of it.

Tears splattered onto the cards. She was not a crier. She was Jacey Steele, and she never cried. Not when she broke both her ankles on her bar dismount. Or when she dislocated her shoulder on vault, or fractured her back and lost her chance at Olympic gold. And definitely not when the team she coached betrayed her and left her with nothing.

But she wept angry tears now for the little girl who grew up isolated and alone. A lightning strike of fury and confusion permeated her body. Winnie threw the word love around like confetti in her letters, but, if she loved her so much, why had all contact ended? Why would her father keep her from the last connection to her mother?

What could it have possibly hurt to let Winnie stay in touch with her?

Only one way to find out.

She swiped hot tears with the back of her hand and found her phone. A fortifying breath helped to steady her. It had been years since they'd had anything that remotely resembled a civil conversation. Since her legal trouble, he hadn't wanted to touch her with a ten foot pole.

Jim Steele's voice clipped through the line. "Well, well, well, I wondered when I'd hear from you. Do you think I'm going to help you? You made this mess, Jacey, and now you must clean it up."

She ignored the sting of his dispassionate words. She was used to them. "Guess where I am."

"I have no idea. Hopefully, at an attorney's office trying to clear up this humiliating legal situation."

"No. Guess again." The ice in her words surprised her. She never stood up to him. She either acquiesced or she avoided. That was the easiest way to deal with her father.

"I don't have time for games, Jacey."

"I'm at Aunt Winnie's house."

Silence.

Then he let loose a string of curses. When he wore down, he drew in a long, weighted breath. She knew exactly what his face looked like in that moment. She'd seen it her whole life. Eyes narrowed, lips flat, three horizontal lines creasing his forehead. When he finally spoke, his superior tone turned her stomach. "How did that lunatic get in touch with you?"

"She didn't. Her attorney did. Winnie passed away last week." For the first time since she found out about her long-lost aunt, a tiny sliver of pain accompanied the words.

"Winnie's dead?"

"Yes."

"How did I miss the heavens opening up to receive Saint Winnie?" His bark of laughter cut through her ear.

She pulled the phone away from her head. Coldblooded, even for him.

"I was going through her desk and found a stack of cards and letters marked *Return to Sender*. They were all addressed to me." She waited to see what he would say, but he remained silent. "Why, Daddy?" She despised the tremor in her voice.

"Why? She hated me, and I can assure you the feeling was entirely mutual. From the moment I met your mother, Winifred had her nose constantly in our business. *He doesn't treat you right, Leah. He has a terrible temper, Leah. He's too hard on Jacey, Leah.* Night and day she nagged, and never shut up."

The room swirled again. Couldn't he see this wasn't about him?

"But what about me, Daddy?"

"What about you, Jacey?" His irritation bled through every word.

"Couldn't you have put your feelings aside for me? I was a little girl when mother died. I needed my family."

"You didn't need that woman in your life or in your career. She was poison. I hold her personally responsible for your mother's death."

"What do you mean? She had cancer. No one is responsible for her death."

"Winnie is." Pain and anger seethed through the line, a pulsing and almost touchable burst of hurt. "I wanted to take your mother to a clinic in the northeast. She wanted to take you and go to Cardinal Point first. She wanted to see her sister. By the time she got back, she was too weak and didn't want to go for treatment."

"She was sick, Daddy. She wanted to see her family. You had to know she was beyond medical help at that point."

"No, Jacey, you don't give up and die. You fight. It was Winnie who convinced her to go out on her own terms. To, how did she say it? ...*die peacefully at home and go to the arms of Jesus* or some religious mumbo-jumbo. Your mother gave up. She was easily swayed by her crazy sister. I didn't want her brainwashing you, too."

"That doesn't make sense. She was suffering. I don't think Winnie forced anything on her. No one else can decide that."

"Well, I fixed her. Once your mother died, I never had to associate with the hair-brained, meddling, condescending, holier-than-thou Winnie ever again."

"What do you mean you fixed her?"

"That B&B you're all worked up about."

"Yes, what about it?"

"Your mother and I owned three-fourths of that. We bailed it and Winnie out of tax and financial trouble. That religious freak couldn't manage her own affairs. I took care of it with one stipulation."

Jacey didn't even need to hear him say the words. "You bartered me against a B&B?"

"Sure I did, and I'd do it again. I didn't want her in your life. She didn't want to lose the house. It worked for both of us."

It didn't work for me...

Jacey groped for answers. She knew what kind of hard-nosed man her dad was, but, by all glowing accounts, Winnie didn't seem like the kind of woman who'd turn her away in exchange for a house. The *Return to Sender* pile told a different story, and she suspected the truth lie somewhere between the lines.

"Yeah, I fixed her," her dad repeated as though proud of himself. Proud he'd taken her aunt away from her?

Then a bigger light bulb went off for her. The brightness blinded her just before it burst and shattered into a million pieces throughout her brain. Truth and clarity leveled in her head. It aligned with a snap and she knew. Her father was broken. She'd always taken his word as gospel, and his opinion ruled her life. But now she saw, with absolute lucidity, that it had always been about him. Any attempt to make him to understand how his selfishness robbed her of something precious was futile. It was a freeing moment and a magical one in which her father's mental power over her snapped and the spell began to break.

She could breathe.

"Good-bye, Daddy."

"What? Do not hang up on me, Jacey. I want to discuss your—"

She stabbed the disconnect button.

For the first time in her life, she didn't give one flip about what Jim Steele had to say.

☾☙

Cole cut through the alley behind the Cardinal Point city offices and slipped in the side door. With any luck at all, there'd be an envelope at the desk with his and Shane's Christmas parade assignment inside, and he wouldn't have to spend any more time than necessary amid CPPD's finest. Not that he didn't have friends there, but every trip down memory lane with the older guys reminded him he would never be an officer like his parents and grandpa before him. And every minute in the lobby brought him face-to-face with the haunting, life-like portrait of his mother in uniform—Cardinal Point's first female officer, and the first to die in the line of duty.

When the nostalgia wasn't getting the best of him, the youngest cops in the department who thought too much of themselves and too little of anyone else, seemed to view his lowly security company with disdain. He was in no mood for that today. Too bad for them, anyway. With the community growing and the budget tight, officials used him and Shane more and more for added security at large events. Yeah, they'd probably be guarding port-o-cans at the float staging area, but hey, city paychecks kept the lights on.

He snatched his envelope from the edge of the information counter in the main entrance and nodded at the girl behind the desk. "Thanks."

"Sure thing, Cole. See you at the parade."

He'd expected those usual feelings when he drew the short straw with Shane and had to go by the station before six. What he didn't expect as he made his way back across the square was to spot Jacey Steele slumped against a bicycle rack in front of Ella's Creative Play with her face buried in what looked like a tub of ice cream.

She had two spoons.

He did a double-take, but he'd recognize that tight, muscular body and pert little nose anywhere. The sissy-dog confirmed it when he came into view from no doubt taking a whiz on Ella's potted poinsettias near the door. "Really, Moe? The Christmas display?"

He headed her way—more curious than anything—because he couldn't reconcile the determined, physically fit athlete he'd caught a glimpse of that morning, with the ice-cream-snorting heap he saw now.

Red and green twinkle lights flickered to full brightness as the winter sun made a quick escape and early evening settled on the street. Shoppers paused to watch strolling carolers as parents ushered children past the velvet rope to meet Santa for his last appearance on the square that day.

And there was Jacey Steele, her gaze fixed on the blonde Sugar Plum Fairy doll in the window, her arm securely wrapped around her large container.

"Jacey?"

She peered up at him through tufts of shiny hair that had come loose from her ponytail. "Oh, hey, Cole. How's it goin'?"

"I'm fine. Uh… How are you?"

"Good, good. Never better. Why do you ask?"

"Carbs," he said and pointed. "And I didn't expect to see you again today. Did you get the boxes and get started on what you wanted to do?"

She jabbed the spoon into the melting goo. "Yes, but I need you to come back with me and look at some things."

"Sure." He dropped to the ground beside her, and Moe moved to sit next to him. "But I have to work tonight. I texted I'd come by tomorrow."

"Yeah, well, I left my phone back at Aunt Winnie's." She shoved another glob into her mouth. "Oh, I'm sorry," she said and reached for the other spoon. "Do you want some?"

"Are you offering me Moe's spoon?"

"Yes, but he hasn't really used it."

He shrugged. "Why not?" He scraped some from the corner. "Is this from Little Penguin's Ice Cream Shoppe? 'Cause I don't recognize this uh… bowl."

"Yes. I went in there with the intent of getting a four-scoop cone. But the scoops were so big and I don't think the guy thought I could finish it before it melted all over me, so he offered me a bowl. It was still too small for four scoops and the extra-large waffle cone, so he jokingly handed me the tub he was about to empty." She licked the back of her spoon. "I accepted."

"So whatcha got in there?"

"Peppermint Chocolate Chip and Vanilla Eggnog for the holidays. The other two are Classic Raspberry and Dutch Chocolate Almond."

"Nicely ordered."

"There's also a sample mini-scoop of something called Birthday Cake floating around in there, but I don't like it. Cake should be cake. Ice cream should be ice cream."

Quirky remarks and plastic spoon waving did little to mask her obvious distress, but maybe she'd let him in on the reason for the puddle of sugar and sadness before him. He put his hand over hers and peeled it from the side of the bucket. Her cool fingers disappeared in his palm. She tugged against the contact, but he didn't let go.

"Is it your birthday, Jacey? If so, ditch the ice cream and we'll—"

"No," she whispered. Tears shimmered in her eyes as a string of bright holly berries in a nearby tree reflected in her gaze. She stared straight through him for one intense but fleeting moment, then pulled her hand away and turned to resume her watch of Ella's window. "Not my birthday."

"Look, Jacey," he said and passed his spoon to Moe, "I know something's wrong. What is it?"

Pain swept across her face. Not fast like a summer storm cloud that quickly wets the ground, but instead, slow and mournful, like the scraping kind of hurt that takes a layer of skin and never seems to heal.

"I found my letters in Aunt Winnie's roll-top desk."

He didn't have a clue. "Letters?"

"Yes. Turns out Aunt Winnie knew me and loved me and wrote to me all the time. She never missed a birthday or any other occasion when I was little. She sent gifts. Probably princess coloring books and hair bows and… dolls."

"Wait. You're saying you never got them?"

"I'm saying my father never let me get them. They're marked *Return to Sender* in Winnie's roll-top desk."

Cole nodded. He'd known all along something wasn't right, Winnie never would have ignored family. "What do you think happened?"

"My father happened. I was little when my mom died. Apparently there was some really bad blood between him and Winnie. He decided we didn't need her in our lives."

"You talked to him today?"

"Oh, yeah. He was as charming and supportive as ever—and by that I mean he was a jerk. I always knew he was a jerk, but I made excuses for him. This time, when we talked, I actually heard him. His hateful words and his hidden agenda. For the first time I didn't ignorantly assume he loved me and wanted what was best for me. I heard the real Jim Steele, and I'll never be able to hear anything else."

Cole glanced at the growing crowd on the street as her voice rose. He stood, alerting Moe, who assumed it was time to walk and peed again on the end of the bike rack.

He snatched the ice cream from Jacey's lap and heaved it in a nearby trash bin before she could protest.

The wildcat-stalking-glare she shot him made him think twice about it.

He offered his hand to help her to her feet. She ignored it.

"Aw, c'mon. You know you would've hated yourself if you'd finished that."

She dusted dried leaves off her backside as she pushed to her feet. "Probably, but I don't need a babysitter, and I certainly don't need another man telling me how I feel or what I need or who I should know or, most importantly, how much ice cream I should eat." She yanked Moe's leash from the rack and jogged off.

Well, now he'd done it. She'd already had a terrible day and he knew that. He'd made it worse.

"Jacey, wait."

It surprised him when she stopped at the end of the block and spun to face him. "Yes?"

"I'm sorry about the ice cream."

"It's not about the ice cream and it's not about you."

"I know."

Cardinal Point's second cold front of the week blew in as if on cue and knocked over the Perfect Purl's cardboard sale sign. Moe started a barking rant at the swirling trash and pine needles on the street, and Jacey shivered.

He pulled off his navy work jacket and slung it around her shoulders. "C'mon I'll walk you home."

She tried to give it back. "That's not neces—"

"I know it's not necessary, but sometimes things need to happen because they need to happen. There's not always a hidden agenda. It's cold, it's dark, you're new here, and you don't have your phone." He righted the jacket across her shoulders, even though it swallowed her, and the Cardinal

Point Security Services name and logo landed somewhere about her ribs. "Can I please walk you home?"

"You'll be late for work."

He pulled his phone out of his pocket. "I'm texting Shane. He'll cover for me till I get there."

Town noises faded behind them as bitter wind continued to bite. Even Moe curbed his curiosity and stayed close to them on the cracked sidewalk.

"What about your mom, Cole?"

It wasn't a trick question or an inappropriate one, but it caught him off guard since everything recently had been about Jacey and Winnie and the B&B. Up until that moment, she hadn't been all that interested in his life.

"What about her?"

"You mentioned your father had passed and I know your grandpa's still alive. You said Winnie was like a mother to you, but what about your real mother?"

Again, not a trick question, but certainly one that made him feel like the ground was moving underneath him and he wasn't sure where to hold on. His mother's death was such old news around town that he rarely had to explain it. Everyone just knew.

"She's dead," he said simply. "Killed in the line of duty."

She slowed beside him. "As in active duty? Like the military?"

"No. She was a police officer here in Cardinal Point. So was my dad. I come from a long line of military men and police officers. My mom was the only woman, though."

"Can I ask what happened?"

"She was working an accident. Some other car came out of nowhere and ran her down on the street. Drunk. He actually caused the accident she was working in the first place and was so drunk he came back around. She couldn't get out of the way, but she did manage to push the other innocent driver to safety."

"Your mom was a true hero."

"Yes, she was, and this town doesn't forget it."

"How old were you?"

"Eight."

"What about your dad? He wasn't part of that accident, was he? I mean…that would be…wow."

"No, no. He died years later. That was sudden and unexpected, too. His heart gave out, but he was too young for that. I don't know. Small town and all. It had to be hard for him to go to work every day on the same stretch of road. Winnie said it was hard-living when he was younger and grief over my mom. She was probably right. She was right about most things."

"That explains your military service and your work in law enforcement."

He shoved his cold hands into his pockets and stepped around a disintegrating chunk of concrete. "Hasn't turned out like I planned. I'm a trained peace officer with military experience, but I couldn't have that job when I got home. Cops can't protect people when they can't hear what's behind them or understand orders in the heat of a situation. So me and Shane are trying the next best thing. Prevention, training, investigation…we're finding our place."

Winnie's Christmas display came into view. He needn't have worried about her finding her own way home. The B&B illuminated half a block.

When Jacey dropped the leash, Moe scampered onto the porch and whined to be let in from the cold. At least he didn't stop to water any of Winnie's decorations.

"Thanks for walking me home," Jacey said as she slid off his coat. "And thank you for telling me about your family. I think you're very lucky."

A peculiar thing to say, but he was beginning to 'get' her brand of weirdness so he pressed her on it. "Lucky? You did hear the story, didn't you? Dead parents, hearing blown up in war so I lost my job, Winnie's gone and I no longer have a fianc— Never mind that. How is it you think I'm lucky?"

"Sorry. That's not what I'm trying to say. I told you I don't communicate well—something else I can thank my father for." She kicked the bottom step and leaned against the rail. "What I mean is I admire your perspective. You've endured great loss so you view the world differently and get more out of it because you don't take it for granted. I thought I had perspective because I lost my mother when I was young, too. I thought I at least understood love and loss and family but I don't." A caustic laugh escaped her throat. "I. Don't. Know. Jack."

"You can't beat yourself up about something you didn't know."

"But it's mind-boggling how blindly I accepted everything my father said to me. Do this. Do that. It didn't matter. Whatever he had to say was God's word." She bent to pick up a pebble and threw it into the darkness. "No wonder I totally stink at being around other people. And keeping me from Aunt Winnie? Who would I have been if she had been there to love me?" She raised her hands in a silent, hopeless gesture. "How did I not know?"

"Aw, Jacey, you have to start over now and put all the anger in its place and not let it rule your life. Winnie taught me that. You think it was easy to come home to nothing? I couldn't work and my fiancée dumped me because I couldn't hear. I kept losing everything over and over, but I had my faith and I decided there was something left in this world for me. Believe me, I had plenty of days when I wished I'd died in combat. It would have been easier that way."

"I'm sorry, Cole."

"Don't be sorry. You can handle your dad and reclaim your life. The only difference between you and me is that you didn't know what you lost until today."

She dropped to the top step, pulled her hair from her ponytail, and shook it loose. "My life's a bigger mess than you know." She slid the band onto her wrist. "So someone really left you at the altar because you're almost deaf?"

"Close enough. She called off a perfectly good half-planned wedding with all the trimmings."

"She must be crazy."

Ten beats later they were still cold, still outside, and still living through another one of their awkward pauses. He'd love to believe Annalise was some sort of crazy. That would somehow make it easier to bear. Winnie had said at the time the girl was touched in the head for letting him go. But

Jacey's rapid defense hit him differently. Was it possible she didn't see him as damaged goods?

He zipped his coat. "Yeah, well, I gotta go relieve Shane. I'll help you with stuff around here tomorrow when I pick you up for the dance."

"Wait. Dance?"

"Sorry. Thought I told you. Tomorrow is the Mistletoe Gala at the hotel and all Winnie's friends and my grandpa will be there. They all want to meet you."

"I can't go to a dance."

"Let me start again. I'm not trying to tell you what to do. I'm asking. Will you please go to the Mistletoe Gala with me tomorrow night?"

"No."

"It's semi-formal. Will you please go to the Mistletoe Gala with me tomorrow night?"

"No. I have nothing to wear."

"Nobody cares. Will you please go to the Mistletoe Gala with me tomorrow night?

"I care. No."

He climbed to a few steps below her and reached for her icy hand—a move he knew could easily get him kicked to the bottom. "Jacey, please. I would love to take you to the dance. Will you please go to the Mistletoe Gala with me tomorrow night?"

Her expression softened in the glow of glittery wings from the heavenly host nearby. "OK."

FOUR

Jacey had no idea shopping in Cardinal Point involved spelunking. There were two clothing stores in town. Bella's, that was, according to the waitress at the diner, *high as a cat's back*, and the Garment Garden, which carried seconds and last year's styles.

Translation: the price was right.

The Garment Garden's low ceiling and lack of windows gave her a boxed-in feeling. Despite the drop in temperature, the industrial-sized fan blew as hard and loud as a hurricane, and did little to relieve her claustrophobia. All that combined with the overpowering aroma of cedar and cinnamon made her brain feel too big for her head.

It didn't help that her raw, sandblasted soul still throbbed with pain. The persistent pressure behind her eyes and the heaviness beneath her ribs indicated she was not over her discoveries from the night before. She couldn't find a place for her aunt's letters in the emotional rolodex that flipped uncontrollably through her mind. But the business with her dad was placed firmly in the *pain beyond description* category, with a sub-category of *betrayal that can't be forgiven.*

After her phone conversation with him, the freedom of not being subject to his judgements had been exhilarating. This morning though, fear and heartache pumped through her veins like thick sludge.

For better or worse, Jim Steele was the only parent she had. In the past, when he disappointed her or was disappointed by her, she'd always been willing to give him the benefit of the doubt. Not anymore. What would this new reality mean for her? She had no idea.

She glanced around the small store and noted how dramatically things had changed. She had few indulgences. No desserts for her or sleeping late on the weekends, but shopping was a fat-free decadence she could relish, guilt free. She longed for the sweet smells and brightness of the high-end shops she usually frequented. She loved pawing through the clothes like a lazy cat. Hours of browsing through boutiques and department stores de-stressed her better than a spa day.

Sadly, she wasn't getting that vibe from the Garment Garden.

She cast aside wistful thoughts of cute upscale establishments to concentrate on finding an affordable dress to wear to the Mistletoe Gala.

She couldn't believe she'd agreed to go to the party with Cole. His persistence and kindness had convinced her to say yes. Delight sizzled in the pit of her stomach like hot rocks on a fire. It wasn't a date, but there was no denying her excitement.

She'd emotionally unloaded on him last night. Odd, but she didn't feel weird about it. It had been nice to have someone to talk to about her dad and Winnie. If she hadn't run into him, she might have eaten herself to death.

A smile stretched her face. What had she been thinking? That was more ice cream than she'd consumed in her whole life. She owed him. He'd kept her from finishing the bucket. Good thing, too, or she might not be able to find anything that fit today.

The metal hangers screeched against the chrome rod as she dismissed another of the Garment Garden's offerings. A different kind of screech tore through the air and this one had her name attached to it. She jerked around and found Tammy Patty shooting toward her like a pinball. The woman actually pinged off the racks as she advanced.

"Hey, girl." Tammy had another festive sweater on today. This one was green and featured three little elves sticking out of the top of a red, glittered stocking. Each elf face was a picture of her three kids.

The sizzle in her belly turned to hard, cold boulders. This was where the fashion-challenged Tammy shopped?

Great.

"Hello, Tammy. Cute sweater."

Tammy smoothed her hands down her round belly. "Thanks. I make all my Christmas sweaters. It took me forever to make this one. The girls wouldn't sit still to have their picture taken."

"Wow... That's impressive."

Tammy beamed an exuberant smile. "Thanks, Jacey. So what do you think of the Garment Garden?"

"It's... um... it's kind of cave-like," Jacey whispered and looked over her shoulder for the salesperson.

Tammy chortled. "It is that. It also has exposed florescent lights and those make you look fabulous." She gave Jacey a thumbs-up.

Was she serious?

"I'm kiddin'. What the place lacks in ambiance it makes up for in prices. What are you looking for?"

"Something to wear to the Mistletoe Gala, but I can't seem to find anything. I hate to spend a lot of money for something I have in my closet in Florida." Mostly she hated to spend money.

Tammy squealed again. "The Mistletoe Gala? Who are you going with?"

Jacey turned back to the clothes as nonchalantly as possible. No need in getting rumors started about her and Cole. "Cole asked me to accompany him." She slid a peek in Tammy's direction and saw her eyes grow and expand until she looked like a walleye fish. "We're not... we're just... He knows I'm new in town. He only asked to be nice. Plus, some of Winnie's friends want to meet me."

"Uh-huh."

Jacey didn't like the calculating glint in Tammy's eyes.

"Well, we better find you something fabulous to wear."

"I don't need any help. As I've said, I haven't found anything. I guess I'll check out Bella's." Jacey moved to squeeze by. "See ya."

A pudgy hand clamped around her arm. "Hold up, Jacey. I have a proposition for you."

Jacey's muscles tensed under Tammy's grip.

The pregnant woman released her arm and giggled. "Oh, sorry. That was kind of dramatic, wasn't it?"

"A bit."

Tammy folded her hands under her chin like she was praying. "Sorry. Will you please hear me out?"

The two pleading pools of Popsicle blue eyes snagged a hold of something inside Jacey and refused to let go. "OK."

"Yay." Tammy fist punched the air. "It was obvious yesterday you know a thing or two about gymnastics, and equally obvious I only know the bare minimum."

"Okaaay. Where are you going with this?" Jacey crossed her arms.

"Here's my proposition. If I can find you an outfit here at the Garment Garden for under… "

Jacey did a quick calculation. "Forty dollars."

Tammy nodded. "Forty dollars. Then you'll come and help with our gymnastics program."

"No."

"Why?"

"I'm only in town temporarily."

"I only need help coordinating their appearance in the town Christmas parade. So we're talkin' a couple of weeks."

"Impossible."

"What? That I can find you an outfit or that you'll help with the gymnastics program?" Tammy propped her fist in the general vicinity of her hips.

A difficult task, considering her entire torso had been taken over by a baby.

"Both. I'm very busy settling my aunt's estate and don't have time for another job. Also, there's no way you can find me something suitable to wear here. I've already told you... twice, there's nothing here. Besides, we don't exactly have the same style or body type."

Hurt plowed across Tammy's face. "Oh. All right then." She turned away but not before Jacey saw the damage her words had caused. She took a few waddles toward the door. "It was good to see you, Jacey."

Moe didn't need to tell her she'd messed up and been rude. One more thing to lay at her daddy's feet. She'd learned by example how to cut people to the core with a few well-placed words. A prick of pain stabbed her as Tammy's normal exuberance deflated right in front of her.

"Tammy, wait. I have no filter. I'm sorry. I think your sweaters are adorable for the holidays."

Truth, if she went for those sort of things.

The woman didn't look one bit happier, though. She had to fix this. "OK. If you can find me something to wear, I'll help with the girls at the rec center."

Tammy's demeanor shifted faster than silky clouds on a breezy day. One moment rejection covered her, the next she practically levitated with happiness. "You mean it, Jacey?"

"Yes, as long as you forgive me." Those words tasted foreign, but good, on her tongue, like the first time she ate calamari.

The round woman waved her off. "You know I forgive you. You'll find I don't have much of a filter, either."

There was that smile again, the one that had a mirroring effect on Jacey. For some reason, when this woman smiled it made her want to grab Tammy's hand and skip around in the sunshine. Weird.

Over the next hour Jacey realized Tammy had mad skills. After the third spectacular outfit, the little con artist let it slip she had some sort of degree in the fashion industry and had worked at Nordstrom's as their lead visual merchandiser.

"I loved it, but I wanted to stay home and raise my kids. I only wear these sweaters for the girls. They love them. Here, try this one." She handed a black pencil skirt with a tiny silver thread woven through it and a shimmering silvery, cobalt blue shirt over the dressing room door.

Clothes were always an issue for Jacey because they tended to overpower her small frame. But everything Tammy chose accentuated her body perfectly. This last offering was the best of all. The color brought out the blue in her eyes and made her skin glow, even in the life-sucking lighting. "Tammy, you're a genius."

She preened. "You look stunning. And the best part is the whole outfit only cost thirty-two dollars. Do you have shoes?"

"I have a pair of black pumps that should work." She couldn't tear her eyes from her reflection. She would have never picked the shimmery blouse, but everything about it was fabulous.

Tammy brushed her hands together. "My work here is done. I'll see you at the rec center at three."

Cold dread clamped down on her good mood and put it in a strangle hold. She started to object, but a deal was a deal. "I'll be there."

"Well, I better go. Toodles."

As she watched Tammy's departure, Jacey wondered if an innocent finger wave had ever been more menacing.

⋐⋙

Jacey floated in an azure sea, a warm balmy breeze fanned across her wet skin. The whoosh of waves whirled around her as soft calypso music sang on the surf—

Nope.

Not helping.

Her eyes cracked open and the Cardinal Point Recreational Center loomed ahead of her. A tiny sniff from the passenger seat indicated Moe hadn't missed her unsuccessful attempt to visualize herself out of a nervous breakdown. She wiped her sweaty hands on her yoga pants. "My happy place isn't helping today, pooch."

The dog whined and put his head on her lap.

She leaned her arm on the car door and rested her head in her hand. "Moe, I haven't touched a gymnast since Tara's accident, and I'm not sure I can do it now." Memories of that event ate her alive.

No.

She could not relive that day and hope to exit the vehicle. A huge breath in, then out, like she used to do before her beam routine. She could do this.

OK, Steele, get out of the car.

She clipped the leash onto the dog's collar. "Let's go, Moe. We've got a debt to pay."

When she entered the building, the aroma of cranberry deodorizer and popcorn laced with the faintest hint of sweaty sock hung in the air. Not unpleasant, but she wouldn't look for that particular scent combination at her local home store either.

She'd called ahead to make sure she could bring Moe. They said they'd make an exception for Winnie's niece. Good thing, too, she needed his support. The pup pranced and preened from the attention he received as they made their way through the lobby.

"I'm glad you're enjoying this, Moe."

The blood in her ears thrummed in time with her pounding heart as she entered the gymnasium. The ten or so girls were clumped together in small groups, their squeals and laughter helped to soothe her razzed nerves.

Sort of.

If she could stand unnoticed for a moment to acclimate herself, she might not sweat through her sports bra.

"Jacey!" Tammy yelled at the top of her lungs. "Oh, my gosh! You came."

So much for a stealthy entrance. She forced her lips into what she hoped passed for a pleasant expression and made her way toward Fertile Myrtle. "A deal is a deal, Tammy. I always pay my debts."

Tammy smiled and hopped around a bit in what could only be considered her personal version of a happy dance.

Jacey averted her eyes and blinked several times. She pursed her lips to keep from grinning at the woman. "Don't smile at me, you little hustler."

Tammy shrugged. "Whatever it takes. Besides, I couldn't have conned you if you hadn't already formed an opinion of me and my Christmas sweaters." She gave her a look that dared her to deny it.

Jacey's cheeks tingled. "Touché."

Tammy looped her arm through hers. "No hard feelings. We're even?"

She nodded.

"OK, girls come and line up. I want to introduce you to Miss Jacey."

The gaggle squawked, balked, and walked as slow as molasses at the North Pole to form a zigzagged line. One girl crab walked to them and sat spread eagle.

The lack of discipline floored her. If she and the gymnasts she trained with lined up like this, they would still be conditioning. Her expectations of respect from the teams she'd coached were well known. When called to line up, her athletes stood shoulder to shoulder, eyes forward, and at attention. Anything less was unacceptable.

She opened her mouth to blast the band of hooligans. The process of whipping them into shape started right here, right now. But the crab walker scuttled over and pulled Moe into her lap. She cooed and petted the dog with loving devotion. Her snaggletooth smile was adorable, but not enough to derail Jacey.

"Is he a boy or a girl?" she asked.

"A boy."

"What's his name?"

"Moe."

"Moe," she said on a sigh. "He's the most beautiful dog I ever saw."

Jacey knelt to look the little girl in the eye. "What's your name?"

"Holly."

"Holly, I need you to line up with the other girls." Her clipped tone tolerated no argument.

The little girl nodded.

"Wow, you handled her perfectly," Tammy whispered. "Every day she's a different animal, and she only performs the tasks that animal would perform. It's not so bad if she's some sort of primate, but today she's a crab. What am I supposed to do with a crab? I've been trying to get her to walk upright for the last ten minutes."

"It's all about discipline, Tammy. There has to be a captain who's in control of the ship to keep it on course." Honestly, how had this woman managed as long as she had?

"I see."

She felt bad. Tammy was only filling in for the real coach. No need to be too hard on her. "Don't worry about it, some people are born to lead, fortunately, I'm one of them."

Tammy's smile was tight. "That is fortunate."

"Yes, well…"

Tammy clapped her hands to gain everyone's attention, which was only marginally successful. But the crafty mom had tricks up her ugly, sweater-clad sleeve. She began to speak barely above a whisper. The gang had to quiet down to hear what she said. "As you all know, the Christmas parade is only a couple of weeks away and we've been asked to participate. Miss Jacey is going to help us. She's an awesome gymnast and has coached for many years."

A cold fist tightened around her throat. Someone had been surfing the Internet. If Tammy Googled her, then she knew what happened with Tara and about the legal troubles. If she knew, why would she trust Jacey with these girls? She watched Tammy, but the other coach gave nothing away.

"I want you all to listen to Miss Jacey and do as she says."

"Yes, ma'am."

"Jacey." Tammy stepped back to give her the stage.

"First of all, I need you to get into a straight line. It's important for you to listen to my instructions and you can't do that if you're distracted by your neighbor." Tara's accident had rattled her, but she still knew her way around the gym.

The act of forming a straight line turned into a major production..

"Stop!" Everyone froze. "Put your hand on your neighbor's shoulder. Now look to your left and right. You should only be able to see the girl's head standing next to you." They looked more like a defunct drill team, all spindly arms and lanky legs, rather than a gymnastic group, but at least they were in a straight line.

"All right. I'm going to test you all and see what your skill level is."

Several hands shot into the air.

"Yes?" She pointed to the bumblebee from the other day. Today she wore a cotton candy pink leotard with baby blue stars.

"Um… a test, like a math test?"

"Not exactly. Mor—"

"Or a spelling test?" One of Tammy's twins shouted.

"No—"

"I won the spelling bee at my school last year," Holly, the crab walker supplied.

"That's nice, but I mean—"

"My mom said you only won the bee because you cheated," a tiny girl yelled.

Crabby's fist slammed onto her narrow hips. "I. Did. Not. You big M-E-A-N-I-E."

"Girls." She tried to wrestle back control, but then one of the younger girls started to cry. "Why are you crying?"

"I don't want to take a math test."

She glanced at Tammy.

"You've got to admit, *Captain*, math tests are scary," Tammy said.

"We're not taking a math test, Tammy. It's an evaluation."

"I'm not mean. You're mean." The shorter girl's bun shook as she leaned in. "You stole my princess pillow."

"No, I didn't. Tell her, Carly. I didn't steal your stupid P-I-L-L-O-W."

"She didn't take your pillow. You left it at after school care."

"Why did we have to wear our leotards if we're taking a math test?"

"Can I go to the bathroom?"

Panic rose in Jacey like Jack's beanstalk, it started with a tiny seed and grew faster and bigger than she could handle. She glared at her counterpart who was laughing her fanny off. "Help me." How had things gotten so out of control? She was used to dealing with serious, disciplined gymnasts. Not children with the attention span of a stalk of celery.

A shrill whistle cut through the mayhem. Tammy removed her fingers from her mouth and shouted, "OK. Quiet down. Miss Jacey is going to watch y'all do your gymnastics skills so she can see how well you perform them."

An older girl with glasses kicked the ground. "Why didn't she say so?" She seemed disappointed there wouldn't actually be a math test.

The next forty minutes was spent herding cats, or at least that's how it felt. Thankfully, she and Tammy had Moe to alert them to any stragglers or possible runaways. If she said *stay in line* once, she said it five-hundred times. Not that it did any good.

She did her best to maintain her strict, Ice Queen persona, but after a particular encounter with one of the girls, she finally gave in to the hilarity around her.

"Carly, I'd like to see your pullover on bars." When the child hesitated, Jacey asked, "Do you know what a pullover is?"

"Yes, it's when I pull my body over the bar and end on top with my arms straight."

"Exactly."

Carly chalked her hands and approached the bar. She jumped, grabbed the bar and struggled to lift her hips up and over. She wiggled and wobbled at the top then dropped to the mat."

"Good. Do it again and this time squeeze your bottom." Jacey made notes while she waited for Carly's next try.

The little girl gave it another go, manfully lifting her hips above the bar again. When she got over, she quavered as badly as the time before.

"Squeeze your bottom."

"I can't."

"Yes, you can."

"No. I can't."

"Yes. You can. Squeeze your bottom, Carly."

"Fine." The girl dropped to the mat and grabbed her behind with both hands. "There. But I don't know how this helps with my pullover."

Laughter tumbled from Jacey's mouth.

Carly gave her a murderous look which only made her laugh harder.

Tammy came over to investigate. "What's so funny?"

Carly pointed her finger at Jacey. "She's laughing at me."

"No... no, I'm not. It's—" She snorted and couldn't finish her sentence. She was appalled by her behavior, but couldn't seem to stop.

The little girl crossed her arms over her thin chest. "See?"

"I see, Carly. Why don't you go get a drink? In fact, everyone take a water break."

When their students were out of earshot, Tammy giggled.

"Why are you laughing?" Jacey managed.

"I have no idea. What happened?"

Jacey bent over and rested her hands on her knees and tried to get control of herself. "When I told her to squeeze her bottom, she dropped off the bar and grabbed her bum with both hands and squeezed." Huge belly laughs escaped her again.

Tammy sniggered harder. "I usually tell them to act like they're holding a dollar bill between their buns."

Jacey choked. "Do you want them to grow up and become strippers?"

"Oh, my cheese and crackers, that does sound bad." Tammy hiccupped and her belly jumped.

"From now on, let's say, *make your hiney tiny*. It's more kid friendly."

Tammy wiped a tear from her eye. "Agreed."

Jacey tried to regain control after the pullover incident, but it was a losing battle. Chaos reigned as the circus came to town and staked its tent for a long run.

Tammy slung an arm around her. "Sometimes, *El Capitan*, you have to admit defeat."

"This has never happened before. We got nothing accomplished." She shook her head in disbelief.

Tammy elbowed her in the ribs. "Don't say that. They're all out there grabbing their tushies. You taught them that."

She groaned. "I have no control."

Tammy rubbed small circles on her back. "Don't be so hard on yourself."

"It's the only way I know how to be."

"Well, stop it, darlin'. Nobody expected it to be perfect the first day."

Her father's voice played over and over in her head like overused words on an old piece of paper.

She wadded it up and tossed it away.

"You know what, Tammy? You're right. I'm going home to fight another day."

FIVE

Cole arrived at the B&B later than he wanted. His suit was new— purchased for a rehearsal dinner that never happened—and his tie was borrowed. That would be because of last summer's tomato-staking incident where Grandpa sliced his new ones to ribbons and used them to tie loaded, heavy branches to their respective cages. It was a misunderstanding somehow about what was marked for donation to the Salvation Army thrift store, and what was still under plastic in Cole's closet. Whatever. It hadn't bothered him too much at the time, but tonight, when he remembered he didn't have a tie, it caused a panicked side-trip to rummage through Shane's closet for something suitable. Slim pickins', there.

The real question was how had he let this happen? He must've been out of his gourd to practically beg Jacey to go with him. Sure, she should go and meet everyone. Sure, it was a fun community event. Sure, he hadn't been out in a while. But the Mistletoe Gala? He would be miserable. Between the rumble of the crowd and the thump of the music, he wouldn't be able to hear a thing. Conversation would be impossible, and the ensuing headache would linger for hours.

And… It. Was. A. *Dance*.

A *dance*. He didn't dance. He could barely carry a cup of coffee from the pot to his desk without sloshing it over the sides—yet another result of the combat injury that messed with his ears and his balance. He was getting better, but still. When a woman is asked to a dance, it is safe to assume she might expect him to dance. So, again, what was he thinking?

He was thinking Jacey Steele looked pretty cute as she shivered underneath his giant coat and pulled her bottom lip between her teeth after angry outbursts about her father. He was thinking her hand felt good in his, even when he had to fight for it.

He was thinking he liked to be with her.

He snatched his coat off the passenger seat. "Maybe the whole dance thing won't be an issue," he mumbled to himself.

The door popped open as he knocked. So much for keeping the cold outside. Moe bounded down the stairs, his tags jingling like Christmas bells.

"Hey, buddy," he said and tried to catch the happy pup so he could scratch under his chin— Moe's favorite spot, Cole had discovered. "Where's Jacey, huh? Where's Jacey?"

A muffled voice came from above him, followed by what he thought were clicks and thumps as he assumed Jacey ran around upstairs. She said something he couldn't make out.

"Shhh, Moe. Hold still." He turned his good ear to the top of the stairs. "Are you talking to me?"

"Sorry," she said loud and clear. "Can you hear me now?"

"Yes."

"I'll be down in a minute. I was late getting back here so I'm late getting ready."

"Yeah, I heard you made quite an impression on the girls at the rec center."

A hearty snort echoed down the stairs. "Does anyone in this town mind their own business?"

He didn't bother to answer.

"I've made piles of Winnie's documents for you to look at," she continued. Tackle whichever you want."

The warm glow from Winnie's Tiffany-style lamps cast beams across the braided country-blue rug in the front room. Jacey had a point. Winnie's style lacked finesse and, yeah, he was gonna admit it, Winnie didn't have great taste. Even he could tell that, but he'd never noticed before. In life, Winnie was comfortable shorts and raspberry tea in the summer, and well-worn jeans and a familiar red sweater in the winter. She was pudgy arms that wrapped him in hugs.

She was Christ-like love.

Now she was piles on the floor. *Keep. Toss. Check with Cole.*

He loosened his borrowed tie and pinched the bridge of his nose to keep tears from forming. Grief tended to sneak up on him like that. Years and years had passed since he cried over his parents, but Winnie's death uncorked a storm of renewed pain. Darks clouds seemed to gather and swirl when he least expected it. Scenes like this caught him off guard and, every once in a while, a raindrop slipped from his eye.

He stepped around Moe to grab a stack. "And I've been calling you the sissy."

"Cole? Did you say something?"

Yeah, it was about his luck that she would catch him like this. "Talking to Moe," he said and turned.

Then it happened. He literally felt his jaw drop. Like in some goofy chick-flick when the nerdy guy first notices a woman's body or some such related nonsense.

He'd seen enough good and bad, beautiful and grisly, bright and tarnished, that nothing should surprise him.

Yet, he was the one with his mouth hanging open.

And she was the one standing confident on the wide bottom step with her hands at her side as if she were about to start a floor routine.

"You look beautiful, Jacey. Beautiful."

"Thank you." She grabbed the rail at the tiniest hint of a wobble. "Not really used to these heels."

She should get used to them. They did special things to her already toned legs.

"The realtor sent over a folder," she said. "It has a list of documents we should gather. He's coming back tomorrow to look at the house with me and make some suggestions on how to get it ready to show. It's going to be more work than I anticipated."

Cole thumbed through the pages he'd picked up in an effort not to stare at her little black skirt and shiny blouse—and all the moving parts underneath them. "Sorry I was too late to actually look at anything. Had to make a stop."

"Maybe we can start when we get back tonight. There's so much to do. All this stuff... I have no idea what we're going to do with it all."

He nodded toward the desk. "Is that the *Return to Sender* pile?" He didn't know why it was important, but all at once it was. That little bundle of a secret life somehow tied them all together as neatly as the black loopy bow that sat on top of them.

"Yep. That's the one. Winnie's letters. Anyway," she said as she pulled a black sweater out of Winnie's coat closet and headed for the kitchen, "I promised myself I wouldn't let that bother me tonight. C'mon, Moe-Moe, hop in your crate." She turned to Cole and put her hand to her face like she was trying to keep the dog from hearing her. "He's really good, but I don't want him gettin' any ideas about shredding a pillow while we're out."

Moe let out a whimper as the kennel door closed with a squeak. Cole hadn't moved since she came down the stairs and stunned him. He finally managed to peel his feet from the floor and walk like a baby giraffe to meet her at the door.

Spots of light danced on her cheek from a pair of dangly earrings that peeked through her hair when she moved. "Those are Winnie's earrings."

"Yes." She stepped back and reached for her ear. "Is that OK?"

"Of course it's OK. She's your aunt. They're yours."

"I didn't feel right at first going in her room, but once I found those letters I felt more connected. I wasn't trying to snoop, but I realized I didn't have the right jewelry and these are perfect. They were sitting in a tray right on top of her dresser."

"Right on top? Out in the open?"

"Yes, why? "

"They weren't in a little pouch or a box or something?"

"No, they were in that tray with a pair of glasses and a tube of hand cream and some other stuff. If you don't want me to wear Winnie's costume jewelry I won't—"

"No, you can wear what you want."

"Then what's the problem?"

"Those are real diamonds and sapphires, Jacey. They're worth a lot of money. They should've been in a safety deposit box or something. Not out on the dresser where guests could've taken them."

Her eyes widened. "They had a layer of dust on them," she whispered. "I wiped them off with glass cleaner."

Cole laughed. "They sure do shine."

"I thought they were really heavy. The stones are huge. Where did she get them?"

"Well, her father—your grandfather—gave them to her. Sapphires are her birthstone. I only know this because she wore them in September and we talked about it once. She told me he invested in things like jewelry, gold, and coins rather than paper."

Jacey shrugged. "I wouldn't know. He died before I was born."

Cole clicked off a couple lights and reached for the door. "Didn't he give the same thing to your mother?"

"I guess not," she snapped. "Apparently you know more about my family's gigantic gemstone legacy than I do."

She stomped outside and made quick but careful steps toward the car. She flung open the door. If she were one bit stronger, it would have flown off its hinges. Once inside, she wrestled with the seatbelt like a crazed kitten in a tangle of yarn.

Cole locked up and took his time getting in beside her.

So she'd cool down and all…

"Sorry," she said as he closed the door. "It's not about you, blah, blah, blah. I know I have to stop doing that."

"It's a stressful time." He started the engine. "I get it."

"How are you so nice about this?" She rested her hands together in her lap, but still tapped out an angry rhythm with her thumbs. "I mean, if I'm being a brat, tell me I'm being a brat. I can handle that."

He chuckled at her sideways logic. "I'm not going to call you names, Jacey, but I thought you said you weren't going to let your father ruin this evening."

She met his gaze across the seat. The earrings swung with her hair and sparkled in the faint light. "You're right. I'm not. I'll get up tomorrow and decide how I'm going to confront him about my mother's things. If there are mementos meant for me, I want them, but tonight is about the dance."

Right. The dance. That thing he didn't do, but invited her to do with him.

He put the car in reverse and stretched his arm along the back of the seat. She glanced at him again. A slight smile came from somewhere inside her. He could see she was trying to retrieve it from whatever place in her heart her father hadn't strangled. A calm and happy Jacey was in there somewhere and she was trying to smile at him.

She managed to pull it off.

And suddenly he felt a little more like dancing.

ೞೞ

Jacey gaped at the splendor around her. "Oh, wow. This place is gorgeous."

Hardwood floors gleamed under crystal chandeliers that hung from copper inlaid ceilings. A mahogany registration desk sat in the curve of a greenery and poinsettia draped banister. Lavish floral arrangements rested atop antique tables scattered around the lobby.

Cole helped her shrug out of her sweater. "The Historic Hollister is the oldest hotel in Cardinal Point, heck, in all of central Texas. It's named after George 'Raider' Hollister, a local Texas independence war hero. Roughnecks from the oil fields and presidents have stayed here at one time or another."

"Hollister? Where have I seen that name before?"

Cole handed his coat and her wrap to the girl behind an ornately carved counter. "The bank on the square. Hollister and Sons National Bank."

"That's right. So they own the bank and the hotel?"

"No. A Hollister hasn't owned the hotel since the early seventies. Coop Hollister owns the bank."

He grinned down at her and the butterflies frolicking in her stomach since he'd picked her up now began to jitterbug. A stream of pleasure flowed up her arm like water over river stones when he wrapped his large hand around hers and led her to the ballroom.

She gasped as she took in the space. "Oh." Because of gymnastics, she'd never been able to go to a school dance or prom. This place was all her girly fantasies come to life.

Thousands of twinkle lights hung like falling stars from the ceiling and cast a romantic glow. Green boughs of garland, dotted with red Christmas balls, looped the walls of the room. The real spectacle was the twenty-foot Blue Spruce at the end of the hall, expertly decorated with a massive star on top and hundreds of gifts piled underneath.

She breathed out. "Magical."

"What?"

She turned to him. "I'm amazed at the beautiful decorations."

"Yeah, the town goes all out for the Mistletoe Gala and I'd say this year they've outdone themselves."

"They certainly have." Her words were a whisper. "Are all those gifts real?"

"Yes, the gala is a fundraiser for Cardinal Point Ministries. The gifts are for area kids."

"I…I didn't know. I don't have a gift." She could hear the panic in her voice, but she hated to look foolish.

He drew her to his side. "I made a donation and put both our names on it. It's all good."

"Oh." She chewed her bottom lip. "That was very nice. Thank you."

His gaze on her mouth, and his thumb rubbing little circles on the top of her hand turned her bones to marshmallow.

"There's Grandpa and Shane. Come on, they want to meet you."

"Why?"

"Why, what?"

"Why do they want to meet me?"

His laughter circled and curled up like a new puppy inside her. "Grandpa knew Winnie her whole life, and Shane's my partner. He's heard a lot about you."

The two men stood at the perimeter of the crowd, one gray and distinguished with a playful glint in his eye. The years had been kind but hadn't left him completely unscathed—if the cane and the slight tilt of his posture were any indication. The All-American, good-looking guy beside him was probably the hometown football star in his day. Both smiled as they approached.

"Cole, my boy." Mr. Boudreaux raised his voice and leaned toward Cole's better ear.

He threw his big arm around his grandfather. "Hey, old man."

"Bite your tongue, son." He glanced around as if making sure no one had heard the declaration. "I don't want you ruining my prospects for tonight."

Cole groaned and Shane laughed. Jacey didn't know what to do so she stood stock still, holding Cole's hand like a life preserver in rough seas, which was exactly how she felt in social situations.

Shane clapped Cole on the back. "Mr. B., you have more dates than me. What's your secret?"

"I think Cole's the one you should be askin'. He's here with the prettiest girl in the room." Mr. Boudreaux reached for Jacey's hand, brought it to his lips, and kissed it. "I'm Lieutenant Colonel Virgil Boudreaux, my dear."

She smiled when he winked at her. "I'm Jacey Steele."

"Oh, geeze. You're pouring it on thick tonight, aren't you, Grandpa? You haven't been in the army for forty years."

Virgil drew himself to his full height. "Respect your elders, boy. Once an officer, always an officer."

Cole snorted. "You mean once a flirt, always a flirt."

"Jacey, I'm Shane Calfee." He extended his hand.

His melting chocolate eyes and easy smile immediately put her at ease. "Nice to meet you."

Cole drew her closer to his side. She felt his body go taut when the DJ fired up the music. Did he not like the song? Did it remind him of his ex-fiancée?

"Are you OK?"

"Sorry? What did you say?" He studied her face.

She guessed the music was simply too loud for him to hear anything else. "Nothing."

Shane greeted a man in a very expensive suit. "Graham Hollister. How the heck are you, man? I thought you were living in Houston."

The sides of the guy's mouth turned up, but not really in a smile. "Yes… well. Unfortunately, I am back in Cardinal Point for the foreseeable future. I'm at the bank now."

Virgil leaned on his cane. "I was real sorry about your dad's stroke, Graham."

Graham's lips flattened and he nodded.

"We sure do miss him at early morning coffee." Virgil seemed to miss the fact that the banker didn't want to talk about his father. "How is Coop doin'?"

"Why, yes, Graham. How is your father doing?" A lovely, olive-skinned woman with a mane of curly black hair joined the group with Tammy at her side. Her hostile stance screamed there was a whole story behind the innocent question.

"He's fine," Graham said, never taking his narrowed eyes from her.

The gorgeous lady hitched up her chin and directed a frosty glare toward the well-dressed man.

"Shane, Cole, Mr. Boudreaux, it was good to see you again." Without a backwards glance, he walked away.

"Well, that was awkward," Tammy said, never one to let a tense moment pass quietly. Then she looped her arm through Jacey's. "You look amazing."

The irony that she, a person who wasn't used to and didn't particularly care for being touched, had a death grip on Cole's hand while Tammy clung to her other arm, wasn't lost on Jacey. The weird thing was, she really didn't mind.

"Thank you, Tammy. You look amazing, too." She wore a tasteful black dress with tiny pearls around the neck and an empire waist. Her red hair was piled on top of her head, with curly tendrils that fell around her face.

"Stop it." The round woman slapped Jacey's arm.

What? Jacey couldn't image what she'd said wrong, and her confusion must've shown on her face.

"I'm kidding, silly. You can never tell a pregnant woman she looks pretty too many times."

"Oh… OK."

"I want you to meet my good friend, Caroline. Our girls are besties. She's the director of the skilled nursing center here in town. "

"Nice to meet you, Caroline." Jacey tried to shake the woman's hand, but unless she was willing to wrestle her arm free of Tammy's anaconda grip, it was no use. Instead, she smiled and nodded.

Caroline opened her mouth to speak, but Tammy had already started talking. "Evidently she isn't Graham Hollister's BFF."

"Would you like to dance, Caroline?" Shane asked, swooping in to rescue her from more awkwardness.

"Yes, thank you." Her brilliant smile rivaled the room's sparkling decorations, but it didn't quite reach her eyes.

"I better go find that good looking cousin of yours, Cole," Tammy said.

Cole didn't respond.

Jacey squeezed his hand and he glanced down at her. She raised her voice above the crowd. "Tammy's leaving to find her husband."

"Oh." He bent and kissed Tammy's cheek. "Good to see you. You look beautiful."

Tammy teared up. "Oh, you big idiot. You're going to make me cry."

Cole laughed.

Virgil took a step and then paused to set his cane in position. "I'll come with you. I want to talk to that husband of yours."

Cole smiled after the two. "Thanks for that. I didn't hear her at all."

She waved him off. "No problem. Would you like to sit over there?" There were tables set up behind the speakers, and she thought it might not be so loud.

"No. I'm fine."

"Are you sure? I don't mind." She faced him so he could see her speak. He watched her lips intently. It was unnerving, and if she were honest, thrilling to be the object of his focused attention.

"No." The reflection of the red lights looked like a banked fire in his green eyes. When his gaze settled on her, the fire flared and began a slow burn inside her.

"OK."

"You should dance. I know Shane would love to dance with you."

She spoke slowly and clearly so he wouldn't misunderstand. "I'm not interested in dancing with Shane."

He glanced at the couples on the floor. "You look too pretty to not be out there enjoying yourself."

She clutched his hand. "I am enjoying myself."

"Don't you like to dance?"

"I might, but—"

"All right, you convinced me. Let's dance." He took a step toward the floor.

She dug her heels in and grabbed his arm with her free hand. "Wait. I did what?"

"Come on. It'll be fun."

"Have you danced since you lost your hearing?"

"Does alone in my bedroom count?" The little crinkles at the corner of his mouth when he smiled nearly did her in.

She couldn't stop her own grin. "Not really."

"Then, no. By the way, me being deaf isn't the biggest problem, it's my two left feet. But if you're willing, so am I." He gave her another of those bone-melting looks. "I might make a fool of myself, but I'd like to dance with you."

The hard, driving rhythm slowed to an easy melody. He pulled her to the middle of the crowd, beneath the huge disco globe decorated to look like a giant ball of mistletoe with red ribbons tied at the top.

One hand went around her waist. The other lifted hers in a classic dance stance. "Put your arm around my neck, Jacey."

She'd be happy to, as soon as her world got back on kilter. Why would he do this? No one had ever put themselves out there like that to make her happy. She would never consider doing anything she wasn't positive she could do, and do well. Especially in public.

He's doing this for me.

She slid her trembling hand around his neck and tried to will away the tension in her muscles. She was as rigid as the Tin Man.

"Relax, I've got you." The arm around her waist tightened, and they began to sway.

She gave a jerky nod and kept her eyes trained on the tie clip in the middle of his chest. Liquid heat coursed through her veins. It burned the awkwardness away. Being in his arms was Christmas, Valentine's Day, and her birthday all at once. Bubbles of delight floated in her belly. Still, she kept her eyes trained on the tie clip. If she raised her face, he'd see how over the moon affected she was by his nearness.

"Jacey," he whispered. "Look at me."

Helpless to resist, she raised her gaze and knew her life would never be the same. His mouth kicked up on one side, revealing a small dimple. His onyx hair fell over his forehead. And his...

She read somewhere the sun was a green star. Looking into Cole's emerald eyes, she knew it was true. They blazed. For her.

He lowered his head slowly as if to give her the chance to stop him. She appreciated him being a gentleman, but stopping him was the last thing she wanted.

When their lips met, she didn't hear fireworks, or choirs of angels, or crashing cymbals. Instead, she heard a small click like two puzzle pieces connecting.

His hand flattened on her back, and he brought their joined hands to his chest. He deepened the kiss and she was a goner.

When he drew back, his face said a thousand things. Wonderful things, thrilling things, things she didn't understand.

The song ended. The DJ took a break. But still they held each other and continued to sway. Could he hear the song was over? It didn't matter. She loved being in his arms.

After several minutes, she reluctantly patted his back. "Cole, the song is over."

He kissed her temple.

"I know."

SIX

Jacey's left eye popped open in time to see Moe's tongue coming straight for her face.

"Ewwwww…," she said after his morning greeting, "that was more disgusting than usual."

The dog circled and came back for another sloppy lick.

"Seriously, pooch, stop it. Go wait by the kitchen door."

Moe tilted his head as if he understood, but he didn't bother to go anywhere.

She rolled over to steal a few more minutes. Rare was the morning she was still in bed at eight. Years at the gym had trained her body to hop out of bed at five-thirty a.m., ready to go. Not this morning. This morning she wanted to contemplate the night before and remember each word, each step, and each breath she took in Cole's arms.

Aunt Winnie's sapphire and diamond earrings caught the morning sunlight and winked at her from the night stand. She smiled as she rehashed every moment. From the second he took her hand to the instant he kissed her, her heart had done extraordinary things. Not even with the chance to make the Olympic team on the line had she experienced such a pounding in her chest.

First, a mere flutter, then, actual palpitations, like a goldfish that leapt from its bowl and flopped around on the counter.

All because of that kiss.

That kiss…

Moe's cool nose tickled at her neck. "I'm getting up," she growled.

Bones creaked, joints popped, and muscles complained as she padded her way down the stairs and across the house. Moe picked up the pace and then couldn't slow down. His too-long nails skated on the slippery floor, and he slid out the door when she opened it.

"Oops… Well, you were the one in a hurry."

He tossed her the doggie equivalent of a stink-eye.

She started coffee, set out dog food, and sat at the table.

Now. About that kiss…

It wasn't as if she hadn't been kissed before. There was that clumsy make-out session with a boy at the gym, and a few passing relationships through high school. As an adult, she'd dated a soccer coach from a rival college, but her profound social and romantic inadequacies brought that to a screeching halt. She didn't know how to play the flirty games or be the girly-girl and bat her eyes at the right time. Like all other men in her life, the coach was more enamored with the idea of *Jacey the gymnast* than *Jacey the actual woman* who was deceivingly vulnerable, chocked full of baggage and flaws. He never looked at her with simple admiration or took her hand for no reason, and he never understood what she didn't say. He didn't know her and probably didn't even like her...

And he never kissed her like Cole had.

There went her heart again, jumping like that goldfish from the bowl and twitching its way around her rib cage at an irregular rate.

"Stop that," she said and thumped her chest. "It was just a kiss."

Moe pawed at the door. She stepped onto the porch to suck in fresh, cold air. "I'm losing my mind, Moe. I've never had so little control over my body. You should stay close by in case you need to go for help."

Moe charged for his bowl.

"I was talking to you," she called after him as her phone chimed in her pocket. She checked the name. "I'm serious, Moe. This call could finish frying the electrical impulses in my heart. I could short-circuit." She shivered and rushed inside toward the coffee pot as she answered. "Good morning, Tammy."

"Welllll, good morning, pussycat," she sang through the line. "I guess you've been lickin' your whiskers this morning after last night's sampling of the cream."

"I don't even know what that means, Tammy." She poured coffee into an oversized Santa mug.

"Settle down, darlin', I'm teasing you. I called to remind you about practice this afternoon. We normally wouldn't get together on a Sunday, but the parade's this Saturday. We need the work."

"I'll be there." Hot liquid sloshed onto her hand as she picked up her too-full cup. "I have to do some house stuff for the realtor and I'm going to work out first, but I'll meet you after."

"Sure thing, and I was wondering if I could come by and get you for church."

"Not this morning, Tammy, but thanks for asking."

"OK. And let me say I'm so happy for you and Cole. Couldn't happen to two nicer people."

"Nothing is happening. Cole and I went to a dance. That's all."

Tammy snort-chuckled too loudly into the phone. "Oh, sure, nothing is happening."

"Please don't make a big deal of this, Tammy. Cole and I are friends and co-owners of the B&B."

"You should know my husband saw Cole at the diner this morning. They were both on their way to parking lot duty at church. We get real busy this time of year. Christmas comes and people slink out of the woodwork to talk to Jesus when they wouldn't give him the time of day any other time of the ye—"

"I understand, Tammy. What is your point?"

"Well, Whit reports back that Cole was grinning from ear to ear and had an extra spring in his step. He's a fine man, Jacey, and he's been through a lot. He deserves to be happy. You deserve to be happy, too, and I'm glad the two of you were being happy together last night on the dance floor. It was lovely. So lovely." Tammy sniffed. "I'm getting all emotional. Gotta go and get these kids to church. See you later."

"Bye, I guess," Jacey said to the lost connection.

She returned to the table and set her phone and her coffee within reach. "Tammy's right, you know," she said to the dog. "Cole is a fine man. The best man I've ever known. The only man who ever…"

A tear formed in her right eye. So new to the crying thing, she thought she could hold it in by willing it to not slide down her cheek. A total failure as it wobbled along her bottom lashes and then splashed to her face when she blinked. More followed as sweet contentment turned to sour doubt. In her whole life, no one ever gave her so much in so little time.

No one.

"I think I'm in trouble here, Moe."

The dog responded with a blank stare, and Jacey couldn't even make the words come out of her mouth.

She tried them in her head instead.

I think I'm in love with Cole.

ॐ

Cole parked at the side of the rec center and headed for the gym. His lazy Sunday had turned into a marathon. First church, and then the Silver Foxes invited him to stay for their Christmas potluck afterward because they needed his advice. Apparently, there'd been a rash of muggings aimed at the elderly as they holiday shopped at the mall in the next town. He gave them basic tips for safety, and they offered him a whole pound cake and a bottle of Old Spice from their gift exchange to thank him for his time. He didn't need either. OK, maybe the pound cake. But what he did need was for them to remember him when he and Shane expanded their business to include the sale and installation of home security systems. As the town grew, so would crime.

"Thought you forgot about me," Shane said as he wiped sweat from his face.

Machines whirred while highlights from last night's NBA game flashed on the large screen above them. "Sorry," he said over the rumble, "got tied up at church. Were you there?"

"Nah. Late night. Met up with some friends at the dance and headed out. Tried to get your attention, but you were pretty busy with the hot niece so... yeah. I'm surprised you made it to church."

Cole avoided his friend's gaze and pretended to stretch and check the final score.

"Aw, c'mon, you gotta give me something. I had no idea you guys had gotten so close. When did that happen?"

He glanced around for a free weight bench. "I'm not talking about this today."

"Must be serious."

"It's not anything yet. You'll be the first to know if it is."

But it was everything, and his whole brain had been wrapped around Jacey all day to the point he was surprised he could direct traffic at church or remind the Foxes to get a security guard to walk them to their car if they were afraid.

Her life was crumbling with each new revelation, yet she locked on to something inside him and made him feel better about himself. Strange how it happened since she admittedly lacked the gene that provided social and relational cues. All he knew was she made him feel good. Everything seemed easier... better when she was around. He stood taller, had more confidence, and wanted to smile at strangers at the gala as long as she stood beside him, clinging to his hand.

There was only one way that dance was going to end once he held her in his arms.

And he went for it.

Shane whacked him on the back. "Snap out of it, Romeo. You want me to spot you or not?"

"Would you rather shoot some baskets?"

"Totally. I think there's a game in there later, but it should be free now."

It wasn't free.

In fact, one half of the court was overrun with little girls and tumbling mats. Tammy clapped and pointed in the distance while Jacey conducted one-on-one instruction with one of the taller girls. With grace and concentration, she moved her arms as if to demonstrate the best position to start whatever it was she wanted her to start.

When Jacey caught him staring, she sent him a quick grin and turned away.

He motioned for Shane. "Let's go back to the weights."

"Are you kidding me? No way. We got half a court here for a game of one-on-one. I might actually get you today with the hot little niece to distract you."

"Not gonna happen," he said and it was on.

Several minutes in, Shane was on top, but it was far from domination. The seconds he spent keeping an eye on the other end of the court did slow him down, but not enough to help Shane's weak game. While he lost a step or two because of his divided attention, Jacey didn't seem to miss a beat at the other end or even care he was there. Not when he lost the ball and chased it like a pre-schooler into her territory—where he further embarrassed himself by accidentally kicking it out of his reach—and not when Shane started his lame trash talk and Cole had no biting response. Outside of the slight grin, she hadn't bothered to look his way again.

But someone else did.

From the corner of his eye, he spotted her. Tall, sleek, wavy blonde hair, Annalise was all smiles and waves as she stood near the door and appeared to want his attention. His brain misfired and sent random electrical shocks through his chest. There was a time he would have enjoyed that, but not now. Now it was more like the blast that blew apart his life and set in motion the slow, painful death of their relationship.

That's how he missed Shane coming straight for him. Normally he would've dodged the collision. Not today. He went down hard and slid a few feet before coming to a stop. He wasn't hurt, but everything ached all the same. Of all days, of all places, of all people to ruin his day, his game, and his fresh optimism.

Shane offered a hand. "Sorry, dude."

"Not your fault. I was distracted."

"I saw that. Tried to warn you of a low-flying broom, but it was too late. You OK?"

"Yeah."

"Aw, man, here she comes. Want me to throw water on her or something?"

In true overly-dramatic style, Annalise rushed to his side. "Cole! Are you all right?"

"Yes."

"Let me get some water," she purred.

Shane snorted into his T-shirt.

Cole used the edge of his sleeve to wipe his face. "What are you doing here, Annalise?"

Shane dropped the ball. It took a wild bounce. "I'll be back," he motioned to Cole and took off to retrieve it.

Chicken.

"I'm sorry to interrupt, but I saw you at the dance last night. I wanted to talk but I lost you in the crowd." She touched his back and let her hand slide to his waist. "I realized I hadn't yet told you how sorry I am about Winnie. I know she was special to you. I should've texted or something sooner. Wasn't sure what to say."

Knowing Winnie, Cole was pretty sure she couldn't care any less about Annalise's condolences. Winnie was gracious, but the two women never hit it off.

"Thank you," he managed as a drop of moisture rolled down his neck and soaked into his collar. "See you around."

What else was he supposed to do? He had nothing to say to her. He headed for his towel and bottled water.

She grabbed his bare arm. "Cole, wait. There's something else."

He stopped and pulled away. "What else could there possibly be?"

"I don't like the way we left things. I was hoping we could meet at the diner for coffee sometime soon and talk."

Bright blue eyes begged for mercy. He had none to give and no desire to go find it. "We left things the way you left things, and it was clear what you wanted, so I don't see any point in going through it again."

"I may have been wrong about those things, Cole. My number's the same, but I'll text it to you in case you, uh… deleted me. Call me. Please."

Did that even require an additional response? Could he form one if he tried?

No.

He moved to walk away again and then she was there with her arms around his neck, pushing herself against his sweaty body and smashing her lips to his in an obvious desperate move.

He jerked away from her over-the-top awkward attempt and fought to peel her arms from around him. She held on like a spider monkey and pressed her cheek to his.

"I really am sorry about Winnie," she whispered into his good ear.

Which made him angrier? That she would approach him at all, or that she would use Winnie's death as a means to do it?

Disgust and hurt careened into him with blinding force. He pried her from his body. He pushed past her and didn't look at her again as he turned to escape.

Shane stood like a beacon along the gym wall. His lips moved, but Cole couldn't hear or read what he said. Crimson rage and his twisted insides kept him from comprehension.

"It's OK, buddy, she's gone," Shane said when he got close.

He took a long drink of water. "I'm fine."

"Yes, I know you're fine and ding-dong the witch is dead or gone or whatever, but that was crazy. Have you even seen her since, uh, since…?"

"Nope."

"C'mon. Hit the showers. Didn't you say you had to get to Winnie's anyway to move some boxes?"

"I'm not letting her run me off." He grabbed the ball. "Let's go. I'm not going down on a technicality."

Shane sailed his bottle into the recycle bin. "You asked for it."

His haze of anger cleared as he stepped in bounds. He glanced Jacey's way to make sure she was still there, still busy, and still ignoring him.

Still there, yes.

Ignoring him? No way.

Disappointment slid across her face and her expression faded to blank and impossible to read as she stared at him across the court. Tammy stood by her, patting her arm as her lips formed some not-so-nice adjectives to describe Annalise.

All Cole wanted to do was scoop her into his arms and make her understand the absurdity of what she'd seen. If she only knew how little Annalise meant to him compared to her…

All business and as cool as a February rain, she turned away. "Girls!" She clapped and snatched the clipboard from Tammy's hands. "We need to do it again. From the top."

He had to fix it and he had to fix it fast. He bounced the ball to Shane. "I'm out. You win."

C3880

Jacey wished she had a sports car, or at least knew how to peel out and leave skid marks on the pavement. That's what this situation called for, a true vehicular fit. Sadly, she only had a four-door sedan, was a law abiding citizen, and had never left a skid mark in her life. Not even by accident. So she was left to stew in her own juices while she drove a respectable thirty miles-per-hour from the rec center to the B&B.

Grief thundered into confusion, then churned with dissolution and exploded into anger.

Life wasn't fair.

A bitter laugh shot from her throat. Boy, wasn't that the truth? What she'd witnessed at the rec center proved it.

Cole, wrapped up in his ex-fiancée's arms and her lips all over him.

The same Cole who'd kissed her silly last night.

The green-eyed monster stomped around her chest, bursting every hope-filled bubble it found. She clamped down on the steering wheel until her fingers hurt.

But that's my Cole...

Jacey knew it had been the infamous Annalise because Tammy had been happy to fill in the blanks.

That shallow, bleached blonde man-eater didn't want any part of a man who wasn't whole. Jacey's sense of betrayal warred with righteous anger at the treatment he'd received from the woman he'd loved enough to want to marry. Her foot plowed on the brake at the stop sign as her brain stumbled over the picture of Cole married to someone else.

Everything blurred in front of her, including her future. She was a fool. A big, stupid, naïve fool. So stupid, in fact, it choked her. She was in love with a man who may very well be in love with his ex-fiancée.

The familiar negative and often hateful voice in her head burst from its chains and rattled through her brain.

I told you it was too good to be true.

Did you really think he wanted you?

You'll always come in second...

A horn honked and tore her from the internal destruction. She checked the mirror and saw Cole behind her on the busy street. He motioned her forward.

Great.

She'd been sitting at the stop sign, lost in her unhappiness, while the man she wanted to run away from was... what?

Following her home?

Why? She was just the girl he'd led on last night. Not his beautiful ex, who now, apparently wanted him back. Why wasn't he with her?

Too good to be true, too good to be true, sang her father's ugly voice. *He's coming to tell you it was all a big mistake.*

Pain, not blood, gushed from her racing heart, as she stopped in front of Winnie's house. When she jumped from the car, Cole pulled in behind her. She ignored the gorgeous man behind the wheel and headed for the house.

The minute she turned the key, Moe began to bark. "I'm coming, pooch." She tried to kick the door closed behind her, but Cole barreled through before it shut.

"Jacey."

"Not now, Cole. I need to deal with Moe." She let the dog out of his kennel and took him to the backyard.

She paced along the side of the house. One of Moe's squeaky toys caught the brunt of her frustration when she kicked it out of her way and into the juniper bushes along the fence. Soft scents of pine and winter earth crept to her nose as she brushed against the branches to retrieve it. It filled her head and calmed her a bit.

Until Cole followed her outside.

Moe greeted him with gusto and Cole returned the enthusiasm like the traitors they both were.

Jacey dropped her chin to her collar bone. Even her dog didn't cut her any slack or help her prepare for the inevitable. No time to form a plan, it was game face on, exactly like her father taught her. Cole would say he was sorry, but he was going back with Annalise and never meant to hurt her. She would smile and say OK and never let him see her pain.

It's how she'd lived her whole life.

"Is nothing sacred, Cole? Moe was out for a bathroom break."

"Is that right? I've watched this dog pee on everything in a two mile radius. I don't think he has privacy issues."

She charged past him into the house. "The files I need you to go through are still sitting on Winnie's desk." She filled Moe's water bowl, then made a show of tidying up the kitchen.

"Jacey, will you talk to me, please?"

Her head said to get the ugly words out of the way. Her heart screamed for another moment under the mistletoe.

She yanked a box from the pantry. If she was going down, it would be in flames and she'd be holding on to him. No way, no how, would she make it easy for him to knife her further. "I don't have time, Cole. The realtor's coming tomorrow, and I have a ton to do. Thanks for taking the time to look at those files." She walked out of the kitchen with her head high.

He followed. "That was Annalise at the rec center."

"I know, Tammy told me." Her voice was steady. Amazing, considering her insides were a wobbly mess. She took the box to the linen closet inside the downstairs bathroom. "When you finish with the files, can you take all the garbage out?"

"Jacey. I know you're upset."

She threw sheets and pillow cases into the box for donation. "I'm not upset, Cole. It's more… I'm acclimating. I didn't know it's customary in Texas to kiss one girl then kiss another girl less than twenty-four hours later. You see, where I come from that's not how we do things."

"That's not what happened. You were there, right? You saw her grab me. She kissed me. Not the other way around."

"Really, Cole, it's fine. I'm a big girl and mature enough to accept last night meant more to me than it did you. My bad. I'll get over it. I understand you and Annalise have history. And what we had last night, well, I guess we didn't have anything." She slipped further into the closet and squeezed her eyes shut. Maybe she was flying too close to the sun. Seemed her attempt to make him miserable as he crushed her only hurt her more. She didn't want to hear about Annalise's kiss—no matter what it meant. Her game face slipped away and all she could think about was her kiss with Cole.

Her perfect kiss.

Her only kiss with the man she loved.

"Jacey!" He smacked or kicked the other side of the bathroom door. "Come out of that closet and talk to me. You're wrong about this. You think you know what's happening here because you're stubborn and don't trust anyone. Last night between you and me... It was great."

She poked her head around. He seemed to take that as a welcoming sign and tentatively stepped in the bathroom.

She narrowed her gaze. "So great you rushed right out and kissed another woman?"

A muscle ticked in his jaw as he stared her down. "I haven't seen or heard from Annalise since the day she told me she needed a man who was whole." He ground out the words between clenched teeth. "I wasn't that man."

"And now she's had a change of heart? If she doesn't want you, why was she kissing you like that?"

He clenched his fists in front of his face. "You are killing me right now, Jacey. You are seriously killing me. It was just a kiss. It meant nothing. It was stupid and she started it. It was a meaningless... ridiculous... wish-it-never-happened mistake. Just. A. Kiss."

Jacey heard the *Snap!* in her brain, as clear as a spoken word.

Snap! Snap! Snap! Snap! Snap!

All control, resolve, and reasoning left her brain. Kisses meant nothing to him. Her kiss, Annalise's kiss, anybody's kiss... He handed them out to whoever's lips were within range and they meant nothing. Now she knew, and how dumb could she be?

Insane anger reigned inside her head, so it was no surprise when the bottle of liquid soap from the sink left her hand and sailed by his head.

He hit the ground and crawled out of the bathroom. "You can't be serious," he yelled over his shoulder. "This is not grade school."

Moe barked and made wide frantic circles around him on the floor.

"I don't care," she said and pelted him with Winnie's seashell-shaped hostess soaps. "Do." *Thwack!* "Not." *Thwack!* "Care." *Thwack!* "You made a fool of me in front of the whole town. I thought last night and our kiss was special." She looked around for something else to throw. "But, no. To you, a kiss is just a kiss. A meaningless, stupid, ridiculous, wish-it-never-happened kiss." She launched three rolls of toilet paper and a box of tissues, then dusted her hands across her bottom. "Thank you for letting me know."

He rolled to his back amongst the debris in the hall. She stepped over him.

He pressed the heels of his hands into his eyes. "Jacey, you know I meant Annalise's kiss was ridiculous. Not the one between us. Do I really have to explain the difference?"

"So now I'm stupid? Don't bother rubbing it in. I already feel like an idiot. You should leave. I have things to do. Don't forget the trash."

"She doesn't want me, Jacey," he said and got up. "She just doesn't want me to be happy with anyone else. She used Winnie's death as an excuse to see me. A real piece of work." He scooted soap out of his way with his foot and leaned against the wall. "You know, she even told me one time she wanted kids and that I wouldn't be a good father because I wouldn't be able to hear them. She said I couldn't hear a baby cry and wouldn't be able to find them if the house caught fire. Who thinks that way? Deaf people raise kids all the time. There are devices, precautions…"

Fury cauterized her veins. Annalise ruined everything in the most wicked way. She'd destroyed Cole with her words long ago. Jacey understood that. With a father like hers, she'd grown up on a steady diet of careless, hurtful words, and had, unfortunately, lapped up the vitriol like cake. As she got older, she'd tried not to ingest his poison, but it was always a battle. And now, Annalise had come between them without words, but with a kiss.

Just a kiss.

She couldn't even look at Cole. To do so would turn her inside out. Of course, he'd make a great father. He made a great everything. He was the best man she'd ever met. The problem was, she was not the best woman, and certainly not the best woman for him. What a joke to think he would give up on her and choose Annalise. How silly she was to think she could play emotional games with him. She, who'd thrown things at him in a childish tantrum and was giving him a hard time over Annalise's clearly unwanted and unexpected behavior. She was not fit for an adult relationship, damaged and broken, with nothing to offer. She couldn't even say she had a job to support herself, and certainly didn't need to drag him into her potentially lengthy and destructive lawsuit. He didn't even know about that... It would be another way to fail him. He deserved better and would find it elsewhere.

And she would let him go because it was the only true and loving thing she could do.

She stumbled to the nearest chair, overcome with the weight of her painful conclusion.

He bent to pick up the toilet paper.

"Please leave it," she begged. "Leave everything. I'll deal with it later. You should go now. I'll take care of what the realtor wants for tomorrow."

"I'm not leaving, Jacey. We haven't settled anything."

She winced because it was already done and the ache was staggering.

She held her breath to hear an unfamiliar sound. "Listen. What is that?"

He stilled the bag of trash. "What?"

"Is that your phone?"

He stepped toward the kitchen. "No. That's the land line."

She followed. "The land line? You mean that ugly green phone on the wall in there really works? I was going to take that down."

"I got it." He yanked the receiver off the hook and wrestled with the tangled cord. "Hello? Yes. Oh, hey, old friend. It's good to hear from you." He turned away from her and said *uh-huh* about a half dozen times before he finally formed a real sentence. "No, we insist. You should come. It's what Winnie would have wanted."

He hung up, but it took a while before he could face her.

"What's happening, Cole? Who was that?"

"The McKillips."

"Who?"

"Winnie's guests, the McKillips."

"And?"

"They'll be here in two hours."

"What?"

"They just pulled into town. They're having dinner with friends and they didn't know anything about Winnie. They didn't get my messages. Their computer died and Mr. McKillip has an older phone."

She held the ladder-back chair for support. "No. They can't stay here. You said they travel in an RV, they'll have to stay in it." She could hear the wild hysteria in her voice.

"I told them to come."

"That wasn't your decision to make," she wailed. "This place is a mess. I don't know how to run a B&B. I don't know how to care for strangers."

"We can't turn them away. It's their tradition to spend the week here in December. They shop and visit before the parade next Saturday."

"But Winnie's not here anymore. It's only me and I don't want guests. I'm not Winnie."

"I know." He paced across the kitchen, made a loop, and paced again. "I know. I'm sorry. I couldn't say no. I kept thinking how it was their thing to be here at Christmas. I felt like Winnie would be disappointed if I turned them away. There'll be a *For Sale* sign out there in a day or two. This place will be gone forever... But you're right. I don't know enough about this and neither do you." He pulled out his phone. "I'll try to get them back and tell them it's not possi—"

"OK, wait a second. What would we really need to do?"

"We need one bed and bath cleaned and sanitized, and we need to provide breakfast food. Winnie made everything from fruit and muffins to breakfast casseroles. As long as there's good coffee, I don't think it matters. It's not like we can charge them anyway if Winnie's not here."

"But it's Christmas. I'm packing boxes to trash and donate, not unpacking decorations. Don't they want the whole experience? We don't even have a tree. I mean, you can see the outside lights from space, but there's nothing inside."

"Look, Jacey, I don't think they care. They probably won't even stay as long as they planned. They need a place to sleep and shower, and a break from the RV, that's all. They shop and visit friends most of the day and sit on the porch and drink coffee the rest of the time."

"Let's do it," she said, meeting his expectant green gaze. "But you have to help me. I'm totally serious when I say I don't know how to do this."

"Sure. We can do it." He reached for her. "What made you change your mind?"

She pulled her hand from his warm fingers. She couldn't say it was because of him. Couldn't explain it was because she wanted to help him honor Winnie one last time before she helped

Tammy's gymnasts through the Christmas parade, got that sign in the yard, and walked out of his life forever.

"I simply asked myself WWWD?"

His half smile and the curious tilt of his head made her lose all ability to reason. This last-minute turn of events may be the final act he needed to let Winnie go in peace, but the frenzied pace of their sudden side project was about to bring more close contact than she could endure.

He grinned. "What would Winnie do?"

"Yes, and you're right. I didn't know my aunt, but from what I've learned, she'd want us to take care of this for her. So… We don't have much time. What now?"

Cole snatched a pad and pen from the junk drawer. "I'll start a list and run to the store later. We need to get their room and bathroom done. Supplies are in that hall closet upstairs."

"Got it," she said and headed for the stairs. "I'll get this mess off the floor in a minute. Can you get out the vacuum and straighten that front room? I have all those piles in there. We also have to mop the entry. Moe's paw prints are everywhere."

"Jacey, wait." He closed the distance between them and pulled her into his arms from the bottom step before she could get away.

His embrace took her breath and left her little to do but slump against him and claw at the fabric across his back as he dipped his head to kiss her neck and whisper into her ear. "Winnie would be proud of you," he said and pulled her tight against his body. "Thank you."

She stifled a choking gasp and an avalanche of tears.

Oh, Aunt Winnie... How proud will you be when I break his heart?

SEVEN

Cole crept to the kitchen door and reached for his key. He'd gotten Jacey into this hospitality mess, so it was only right he help her with it. That's how he found himself on Winnie's porch at six a.m. with cinnamon streusel muffins from Songbird's and intentions to make the best pot of coffee the McKillips ever experienced. Then they would move on, Winnie would be pleased from her front porch in Heaven, and he and Jacey could make it over their bump in the road.

He'd do whatever it took.

One look at the kitchen, though, and it didn't seem like she needed any help.

Moe barely acknowledged him from his curled-up position on the rag rug in front of the warming oven. Christmas cups with matching saucers were lined up near the sparkling clean and ready-to-brew coffee pot on the counter. Winnie's muffin tin waited beside sugar and flour canisters on the table as the screen from Jacey's laptop cast light across a pile of blueberries.

Cole set his muffins out of sight and looked to the dog for answers. "What's happening here, Moe?" He reached for a berry.

Jacey's shriek as she rounded the corner stopped his hand mid-air.

"Geeze, Cole, you scared me! And don't touch those. There are exactly two cups." She set eggs on the table. "What are you doing here at this hour? And why didn't you knock?"

"I came to help with breakfast and I didn't want to wake anyone. What are *you* doing up at this hour?"

She raised her hands and glanced around the kitchen as if it were the dumbest question he'd ever asked. "Uh… What does it look like I'm doing? I'm assembling breakfast for our guests." She cracked an egg against the side of a bowl. "Besides, I'm always up at this hour."

Bright pink yoga pants hung well past her feet and dragged along the floor in spilled flour. Her Florida Northern T-shirt hugged her curves and reminded him of the way she felt in his arms. He shook his head to dislodge the image. "I thought you had no idea what to do."

"I didn't, but I have baked a time or two, and that's what the Internet's for. I watched some YouTube. I logged on to The Food Network. I went through Winnie's recipes. I figured anything worth doing was worth doing well."

Normally, he would agree, but he was convinced last night she only wanted to get through the visit. Not enjoy it or labor over it any more than she had to. He leaned against the counter where the sugar bowl caught his eye.

"What are these red and green shiny specs in the sugar?"

"Oh, yeah, I saw that on Pinterest. It's holiday baking sugar. Like the kind you sprinkle on Christmas cookies. Adds a festive touch to plain white sugar and dissolves like the rest of it."

He slid farther down the counter. "Now you're scaring me."

"Stop," she said and pointed at the scraper. "Hand me that, please."

She folded, dashed, pinched, mixed, and stirred exactly like Winnie used to do. Warm memories brought his heart to his throat. "Wow. That technique must run in the family or something."

She dusted her hands and moved Winnie's recipe closer to the computer. After the comparison, she added two more spoons of white powder and looked again. "Honestly, I don't know what happened." Berries tumbled into the creamy batter from her steady hand. "I visited with the McKillips after you left. They went on about Winnie and all she meant to them and how good the house looked even with this mess and about how they love her lemon blueberry muffins... I don't know." She rested her hands on the table as the berries sank. "I sat here with her recipe box... I'm tellin' you it's this kitchen. I feel Winnie when I'm here alone. I *feel* her." She grabbed a scoop and pulled the tin closer. "I know I sound crazy."

"You're not crazy." He swept his hand across her back and paused to massage her shoulder. "You're missing someone who loved you."

"I didn't know her."

"But you have a connection with her here."

"I guess. Either way, the next thing you know, me and Moe were a whole town over at the twenty-four hour superstore."

"You went to the grocery store after I already shopped? What'd I forget?"

"Well, duh, Cole, you can't make Winnie's famous lemon blueberry muffins with frozen berries. Too much moisture. I think that's part of her secret, but I had to go to a bigger store to find fresh produce from South America this time of year. *Voila*," she said and opened the oven door, "Winnie's muffins will be out in twenty to thirty minutes." She swiped a piece of hair from her eyes and gazed up at him. "Don't know for sure because I don't know this oven."

Who was this domestic goddess, and what had she done with Jacey?

From the smudge of flour at her jawline to the single hair that was caught in her lashes, she seemed at home in the very place she was so uncomfortable a few days ago. Her scent, an easy combination of warm vanilla and something flowery, drifted between them and made it impossible for him not to hug her. She was suddenly irresistible, and he didn't see any reason why the twenty to thirty minute wait for muffins couldn't be translated to twenty to thirty minutes of kissing in the kitchen.

He was wrong.

Her hands pressed against his chest as a clear signal to stop. She twisted out of his reach and busied herself with the mess.

"Sorry," he said as he made awkward jabs at the coffee maker in search of the start button. "I, uh…

misread that moment. Thought we were at a different place."

"No, no…" She returned the bottle of vanilla to the cabinet and grabbed a towel to wipe the table. "I just think we need to keep our partnership where it is right now. We need to leave things where they are."

Fear and irritation grew in his gut like a fresh patch of poison ivy. He knew a blow-off when he heard one. Or did he? She wasn't all that clear about half of what she struggled to say. "What does that mean, Jacey? Is this about Annalise? You have to believe me, that was noth—"

"I believe that, Cole. I know what it was."

"Good. So we can move on? Pick up where we left off?"

She pressed the lid onto the flour and didn't even try to look him in the eye. "Like I said, let's leave it alone for now."

Yep. Her version of a blow-off. And yes, it stung far more as each second ticked by. Did he believe it? Not even for as long as it took him to cross the kitchen and take hold of her upper arms. "Look at me, Jacey. What's really going on here?"

"Reality, Cole. That's what's going on." She hung in his grasp as if unable or unwilling to give him anything that resembled hope. Had her father beat her down so far she couldn't try? "I don't live here or even belong here. I have to go home soon. We're stuck in a fantasy. It's not real. We don't even know each other. Do you want to risk everything on one night? One kiss? "

"Maybe that's all it takes, Jacey."

Aged wood creaked and Moe darted for the stairs. Mr. McKillip's booming voice arrived in the kitchen a whole minute before he limped in behind it.

Jacey straightened her T-shirt. "Good morning, Mr. McKillip. You're up early."

"Oh, I don't sleep much anymore, and old habits die hard. Been on a five a.m. wake-up call my whole life. I hung out upstairs and read my book until I smelled coffee."

Cole pulled out a chair for him. "It'll be ready in a minute. Straight up black, right?"

"Yessir."

Jacey rummaged in a cabinet near the stove and pulled out a frying pan. "I'm going to make some bacon."

"Uh, you don't need that," Cole said. "I got that microwavable kind to make it easier."

She set the pan on the burner with determination. "Nope. Only the real stuff for the McKillips."

Mr. McKillip smiled and went back to talking to Moe.

Cole opened the fridge. "I can't believe you got real bacon." He peeled apart the package. "And you're going to fry it."

"I live on a restricted diet, Cole, but I'm not a mole person. I don't live underground. I know about bacon. In fact, America is in the middle of a whole bacon renaissance. I saw a bacon cupcake the other day."

"Those are good. Songbird's has them."

She pulled a clean fork out of the drawer. "I thought as much."

"That's nothing. Grandpa's lymphatic and circulatory systems are literally held together with bacon fat. No one eats bacon like that man. He'd fall over if the grease didn't lubricate his joints."

She shot him a warning look. "That's enough. Grab those eggs. You're in charge of that."

"I got this. You go work on muffins and coffee."

Jacey poured a cup and set it in front of the older man. They'd been coming to Winnie's for years and Cole couldn't even guess how old they were, but this year, Mr. McKillip's eyes had lost a bit of spark. Age had noticeably slowed him to half-speed, and it didn't look like his once broad shoulders filled out his familiar blue flannel shirt.

Cole opened three drawers to find a whisk. "Will Mrs. McKillip be down soon or should we hold breakfast?"

"Nah... fire it up, son. She's moving slow and not feeling well this morning. I'll take her a muffin and a cup of tea in a bit."

"I have over-the-counter medicine," Jacey offered, "or I could get her something."

"Oh, no, that won't be necessary. She has what she needs. For all the good it'll do her."

Cole stopped the fork in the air with a raw piece of bacon hanging off the end. He met Jacey's hesitant and questioning gaze. *I don't know*, he mouthed with a shrug.

Mr. McKillip smacked his hand on the table and raised his cup for a long swig of morning fuel. "Aww, now don't you kids worry. That's good brew, by the way. My lovely better half battled cancer two times before and won. This time, she's too tired to mess with it, but she decided it would not slow her down until it slowed her down for good." He took another drink. "We'll be finishing up our fall trip here and heading home to be with our kids for Christmas. This stop has always been one of her favorites. She's so sorry to hear about Winnie. We had no idea."

Cole tried to read Jacey's thoughts since there was nothing he could tell from her expression. Her mother had died of cancer, Winnie was gone, and now two elderly wounded strangers had shown up in her temporary kitchen in need of comfort and care. She'd made muffins and bought bacon, but could she deliver anything else?

Dig a little deeper, Jacey, Cole silently prodded. *You can do it.*

She stood and took his cup for a refill. "You should stay as long as you like." She gave him a tentative pat on the back when she returned to the table. "If this is where Mrs. McKillip wanted to be around Christmas, then this is where she should be. I'm only sorry Winnie couldn't be here to take care of her."

"Well, thank you, little lady. We'll be moving on after the parade. My wife loves parades. And she always loved to come here because Winnie and Cardinal Point is all about Christmas."

"About that," she said and went to stand by Cole, "we were talking about the tree and Winnie's decorations before you got here. We're sorry we're late in getting it up. We are going to do that today. Right, Cole?"

A sharp elbow hit his ribs. The bacon he was turning dropped in the pan with a splatter. He jumped back. "Yes. Uh... The tree farm? Today?"

She poked him again.

He took the hint. "Yes. The tree farm. We'll ride out there today."

"Yes," Jacey added, "and I already have the ingredients for Winnie's famous Christmas cookies."

Cole's stomach cheered a little. "Muffins and cookies?"

"Yes. We'll do the whole thing. Cocoa, cookies... All the usual stuff. Soon. Like tonight."

"Tonight?"

"Yes, Cole, tonight. I have to be at the rec center in a bit to work with the girls, but we'll get it all done."

"Good!" Mr. McKillip clapped his hands together and nearly sprang from his chair. "I'll go check on the missus and let her know. Be right back. How are those muffins comin', little lady?"

"Any second now."

Cole turned off the stove and transferred food onto plates. "That's an awesome gesture, Jacey. It means the world to them."

"It's the right thing to do. Last night this seemed monumental, but they're just people. People who were important to Winnie. It seems so natural to take care of them."

"Like I said, it's what she would have wanted."

"I get that," she said and set salt and pepper on the table. "And everything I needed to know was in a file. Winnie had menus, shopping lists... She even had a time schedule for when to launder certain things and when to clean and how to prepare and set out everything."

He took the orange juice from the fridge while Jacey set Winnie's Christmas juice glasses at every place. "Well, she worked it successfully for years. She knew how to get it done." He checked the timer and handed her the mitts. "You have her *where there's a will there's a way* attitude. There's nothing you can't do, Jacey."

She held his gaze this time and didn't look away.

He found hope there.

The timer dinged.

Winnie's kitchen does it again.

ೞೞ

"Girls, for the tenth time, point your toes!" The vicious headache behind Jacey's left eye threatened to explode into a full blown migraine. "Every one of you has floppy feet in your handstands. Make your hineys tiny and point your toes, please."

Tammy handed her a bottle of water. "Your teeth are clenched so tight I'm afraid you might break one. Drink this, if for no other reason than to open your mouth and loosen your jaw."

"No, thanks." She pushed the water away while she gritted out another correction.

Tammy thrust the drink her way again. "I insist."

Jacey shoved it back. "I'm not thir—"

"Drink it," Tammy whisper-yelled.

When she saw the little woman's face, she knew Tammy wasn't messing around. She grabbed the bottle, twisted the cap, and drank. Mostly out of defiance, but with the first swallow, the tendons in her neck began to relax.

"Thanks." She slid her co-coach a sheepish grin. "I needed that."

"You're welcome. I thought it was better than a punch to the throat."

The little bully straightened her truly heinous sweatshirt. This one was black and had slits cut out of it in several places to reveal the red tank underneath. Little elves danced around a sickly Christmas tree with mismatched buttons for decorations. The whole thing was topped off with gold cord and fringe on each shoulder, like an officer's uniform. It looked like Charlie Brown's gang got into a knife fight with the French Foreign Legion.

"Nice top," she said and then sucked down more water so she didn't choke on the sarcastic words.

Tammy smiled brilliantly as one of the kids skipped by. "Thanks. If you don't change your attitude, I'm going to make you wear it." The threat in her words was unmistakable.

Guilt wrapped around her. These kids didn't deserve to take the brunt of her temper. "You're right. I'm sorry."

Tammy crossed her arms over her bump. "Don't tell me. Tell them." She lifted her chin toward the group.

That made Jacey pause. It was one thing to apologize to Tammy, her friend, her equal. But another thing to say she was sorry to her students, her team. She lived by the rule that there was a distinct line between player and coach, and it was the instructor's job to make sure that line wasn't crossed.

Be the boss.

Keep the upper hand.

Show no weakness.

Yeah, look how well that had worked out for her.

The hateful expressions of the team she left behind in Florida haunted her nightmares. She never wanted to see these girls look at her that way.

She surveyed the rag-tag athletes and knew Tammy was right. "Girls. Gather around and take a seat."

They traipsed over to her. Their wariness was a mule kick to her chest. "Miss Tammy has pointed out to me that I've been in a bad mood and I've taken it out on you guys today."

She almost burst out laughing when half the group nodded in agreement. Had to love their honesty. Genuine and transparent, there would be no smiling to your face while they jabbed a knife into your back. Not like the team who had betrayed her.

"I wanted to tell you I am sorry and I will change my stinky attitude. You guys deserve better than that from me."

"We forgive you, Miss Jacey," one of them said, and the rest of the group chimed in.

A nod was all she could manage. Their tender, sweet words clogged her throat with raw, wild emotion. She hadn't realized how much she needed their forgiveness until they'd given it so freely.

Tammy clapped. "OK," she said, drawing the girl's attention.

Jacey was grateful for the save. Her partner took over like a seasoned pro.

"All right," Tammy instructed. "Grab a buddy, and each of you do ten handstands with tight bottoms and pointed toes. Hold each other accountable. No flappy feet or bad form."

They stood, paired off and got down to business.

Tammy kept her eyes trained on the girls but inclined her ear toward Jacey. "You want to talk about it?"

"Not really. Bad day, that's all." She turned away and hoped the woman would get the hint.

But Tammy, being Tammy, ignored the hint and barreled forward. "This isn't about what happened with Annalise and Cole yesterday, is it?"

"Not exactly."

Jacey didn't share. Ever. She learned a long time ago, girls couldn't be trusted with her secrets, her feelings, her dreams. But apparently, Tammy was her friend, and she needed a friend. So for good sweater or bad, Tammy was going to get an earful. "Cole and I did argue about Annalise, but... it wasn't really about that. I mean, I didn't like seeing her kiss him, but—"

"Oh, Jacey, you have to know there's nothing going on there. She crushed anything that was between them when she broke off their engagement."

"I know. I also know he didn't want or encourage anything she did yesterday."

"Then what's the problem? It's obvious y'all are crazy about each other. And he's one of the best men I know."

"That's the problem, Tammy. He is the best man I know."

Tammy shook her head. Red curls bounced around her face. "I don't understand."

"I know you Googled me."

Every inch of Tammy's exposed skin turned pink. "Well, yes—"

"So you know how messed up my life is. I have nothing to offer him except a ton of trouble. The poor guy's had enough trouble, don't you think?" She raised one hand, palm up. "I'm the most messed up person I know, and he's the best person I know." She raised the other hand, and then moved them up and down as if weighing what they held. "These two things don't go together."

Tammy nodded and turned her attention to the girls. The punch in the throat she threatened earlier would have been less hurtful than her obvious agreement.

But then, Tammy stepped back, her serious expression a mixture of compassion and certainty as if she were going to share great wisdom or confide to her the answer to an ancient question. "I know exactly how you feel," she said. "I don't even blame you for feeling that way, but I will say you're dead wrong."

"I doubt you know how I feel, Tammy. You have no idea what I deal with on a daily basis. You, on the other hand, appear to have it all."

"I know how that feels, too." She gave Jacey a sad smile.

"What do you mean?"

"I know how it feels to compare your inside with everyone's outside."

Jacey stepped away and picked at the label on the bottled water. "Except for your unfortunate taste in sweaters, your life seems pretty perfect to me. You have beautiful children, a wonderful husband, and everyone loves you."

"It wasn't always that way. I had to learn to love myself before other people could love me. I know it sounds simplistic, but there it is."

"And how did you go about learning to love yourself, Tammy? Self-help books? Yoga? Meditation?" Contempt crept in and crusted each word like soured milk.

Tammy shrugged. "I learned that Jesus loves me." She wrangled her thick mane into a high ponytail. "It took a long time for me to understand how that simple truth could change my life. But eventually, I figured if the King of the World loved and accepted me, warts and all, then I should probably grab a hold of Him and not let go."

Jacey could feel confusion contorting her features. She tried to rearrange them into a semblance of a smile, but didn't know if she hit the mark.

Tammy chuckled. "I can see by your face that's not what you were expecting me to say, and you don't buy it for a minute." She patted Jacey's arm. "That's fine. He loves you whether you believe it or not," she said and walked away.

"Seriously, Tammy? You're gonna Jesus Juke me and then run away?"

Tammy winked over her shoulder.

Jacey's phone vibrated in her pocket. Her attorney's name popped on the screen like a recurring nightmare. "Tammy, I have to take this." She swiped the screen. "Hello, Meredith."

"Hello, Jacey. I'm calling to let you know the date for the deposition has been set."

She stumbled to the gymnasium wall and clawed for a place to keep herself upright. "Yes. When will it be?" A few more steps, and she'd pushed herself out of the noise and to the front glass doors of the rec center. Cole was already there to pick her up to go chop down a defenseless pine. Tall, handsome, and with a smile that would melt concrete, he waved. She stumbled again. Stupid Christmas tree. Whose idea was that anyway? "I'm sorry, Meredith, say that again, please."

"January fifth, at ten a.m. at the office of Tomlin, Jacks, and Nash. Will you be back by then?"

"Certainly, Meredith. I'll be back in two weeks or whatever it takes. I want this settled."

"Oh. I thought maybe you'd be staying for Christmas and New Year's Day and would need travel time after the holidays."

Cole met her gaze, expectant and eager, warm and kind, like a blanket of refuge she could wrap herself in forever.

If only she deserved his sanctuary.

"No. I'll be home. There's nothing for me here."

Cole started toward her as she hung up. Deposition, parade, Cole, cocoa, deposition, deposition, deposition… The words looped through her head as new cold tendrils of dread chased her usual panic through her body and raised it to new heights.

She slid her phone into her pocket. "Hi, Cole. I need to finish with the girls before I can go."

"No worries. We have time."

A sudden, piercing scream rent the air. She burst back through the gym doors, leaving Cole in her wake.

Tammy made her way to the group of girls as gasps gave way to urgent chatter. A small form lay crumpled amidst the cluster. Blood seeped like an advancing army into a pool on the shiny wood floor. Maribeth, one of Tammy's twins, lay near the puddle, crying like she was dying. For all Jacey knew, she could be.

Not again, not again, not again.

Tammy charged into mother mode. "Holly, run and get a couple of clean towels from the front desk. Kari, go find the director and ask her to call my husband. Tell them it's urgent. The rest of you get your things together and have a seat. She's going to be fine. A few stitches and she'll be right as rain."

Tammy's other twin clung to the bottom of her sweater. "What can I do, Mama?"

"Sit here next to me. If you want to help, pray for your sister."

"OK." She bowed her little head and began to pray.

Tammy's calm and soothing tone sent Jacey over the edge. They needed answers, and they needed them now. "What happened here?"

Big, scared, swollen eyes stared back at her, shell shocked. No one said a word. Not acceptable. "I said, tell me what happened here!"

"We finished our handstands first," came a trembling voice from the back. "While we waited for everyone else, Maribeth did a bridge, but her feet slipped and she crashed down on her head. She wasn't on the mat."

Tammy positioned herself closer to her daughter on the floor. "Jacey. It's fine. It's a cut. She needs a couple of stitches."

Tammy's honey-sweet and annoyingly calm words catapulted her to a new level of rage. "It is not fine! She could have a concussion or a brain injury. Is anyone calling an ambulance?" She ripped her phone from her pocket as the girls reacted to her hysteria with more tears.

"Stop cry—"

"Jacey. Come with me." Cole took her arm and hustled her to the side door.

She did not go gently, instead she bucked against his strong arms until he clamped her against his body and stole what was left of her breath.

"I *will* pick you up. Is that what you want in front of this crowd?"

She jerked away as he swung open the door. She stomped through it on her own.

Outside, the blast of cool air did nothing to calm her roiling insides. Instead, black waves of terror sank deeper beneath her skin as she contemplated the possibility of another serious injury to a gymnast under her care. "What do you think you're doing? I need to get back in there. I'm responsible."

"You're not going anywhere near those kids until you get yourself under control." His big body made it impossible for her to flee.

"Calm down? How can I calm down? That little girl is lying in a pool of blood and it happened on my watch." She shoved at his hard chest with zero effect.

"She's going to be fine. Tammy is an experienced mom, and if she's not worried, you shouldn't be worried. The head bleeds a lot, you know that."

She knew. If her rational mind were engaged in this situation at all, she would've already considered that. But pure emotion fueled her tirade, and rational thought was a million miles away. She grabbed two hands full of hair and paced.

"Take a deep breath, Jacey. Those girls are scared. The last thing they need is for the adult in the room to freak out. Surely you've seen worse injuries than this. What's going on?"

"What's going on? I'll tell you what's going on. I no longer coach gymnastics, Cole. And do you know why?"

He shook his head.

She kicked a rock and stood straight to meet his gaze. If she was going to expose herself, she was going to put it all out there. That way, she could see the disdain in his eyes when it became clear she'd never be good enough for him. "Because, two months ago, one of my gymnasts did an unauthorized move on bars and came down on her neck. She's paralyzed, Cole. Paralyzed. That happened on my watch, too. That's what's going on."

"Jacey, I—"

"You want to know what else? I specifically told Tara not to do that skill, multiple times. They were stretching on the mat, and I was getting chalk out of the storage cabinet—right there—I never even left the room. My assistant coach wasn't there that day, so I was doing double duty. I was distracted, frazzled, and she did it while my back was turned. The whole team was there. They all saw what happened. They saw, and not one of the nineteen girls told the truth about it. They let me take the blame. That's how much they hate me. You know why? 'Cause I'm not a likeable person, Cole. I'm cold and I'm mean and I'm terminally unlovable."

A tiny muscle twitched around his right eye. It was the closest he came to a flinch as he remained steady and took the full force of her rant.

"That's not all of it. I've lost my job, I'm being sued by Tara's parents and I've used every penny I have to retain the best civil attorney in Florida. I'm broke. I have nothing. Nothing to give. Nothing at all."

"Jacey, that's not tru—"

"Stop. I can't hear you now."

"That's news to me, considering I'm the one who's deaf. You can hear, but choose not to."

She shoved past him to get inside and check on her girls.

And then she was going to Winnie's.

It was the only place she wanted to be.

EIGHT

Jacey yanked open the oven door. A blast of hot air hit her square in the face and dried the tears that leaked from her eyes. As soon as she'd left the rec center, they'd begun to fall, and fall, and fall. She was sure making Christmas cookies was supposed to be a happy occasion.

Maybe next year.

Moe bumped her leg. His mournful whine only added to her misery. She picked him up and buried her nose in his neck. "I'm fine, pooch. Or I will be. Someday."

She'd done it. She'd told him the truth and now she'd never see him again except as it related to the sale of the B&B. It hurt, but he needed to see why there wasn't a future for them. The sooner he understood that, the better.

With the cookies done, she went to put lights on the tree she'd picked up at the grocery store. It was a pathetic little thing. She hoped the McKillips weren't too disappointed, but it was all that was available. They were nice people. Hopefully, they lived in the *it's the thought that counts* camp.

As soon as she saw it sitting on a small table in the living room, she cringed. It was worse than she remembered. Moe sat in front of it, his black head tilted to one side as if he was trying to figure the ugly object out.

It was barely four feet tall with gaps in the branches big enough to stick her arm through. Between that, the brown patches, and a distinct list to the left, there was no way was she pulling this off.

"Step aside, Moe. I will not fail at one more thing today."

She grabbed the string of lights she'd stolen from the toy train on the porch and began to wrap. Unfortunately, it looked more like a badly bandaged head wound than a symbol of Yuletide joy. There really wasn't any way to make the tree look good.

Three loud bangs on the door jarred her from her stupor and sent Moe on a barking spree. Cole didn't wait for an answer, but strode in carrying the biggest, fullest tree she'd ever seen.

"Move that chair for me, will ya, Jacey?"

She slid the heavy chair from side to side to get it out of the way while Moe made a fool of himself trying to impress Cole with his high-pitched yipping.

"Can you grab the stand from the porch and set it right here?" He tried to avoid the dog while maneuvering the massive tree through the great room. "Sit, Moe," he commanded. The dog immediately dropped his bottom to the floor with his mouth open, tongue lolling.

"Why are you here, Cole?"

He dropped the Virginia Pine into the stand and peered at her from the other side. He hiked one dark brow as if teasing her.

"OK, of course I can see you brought a tree, but why did you bring it?" She picked at one of the needles as he stooped to secure the trunk in the base. "I didn't think I'd see you again today."

He peeked at her through the dense branches. "Jacey—"

"Mmm-mmm, something sure smells good," Mr. McKillip shouted from the foyer.

Jacey turned from the awkward exchange as her guests strolled into the room. "Mr. and Mrs. McKillip, how was your day?"

Mrs. McKillip dropped onto the loveseat in front of the tree and smiled brilliantly at Jacey. Moe jumped up next to her and dropped his head into her lap. "We had the best day. First lunch with old friends in town and then the tree farm for a hayride. The weather couldn't have been better. Just cool enough to snuggle with your honey." She smiled at her husband. "Like I said, the best day."

Mr. McKillip took his wife's hand and raised it to his lips. Love and respect poured off him in waves of barely restrained sadness. "Every day with you is the best day."

Jacey needed to avert her eyes from the scene or risk bursting into tears, but she couldn't wrench away. She never knew this kind of devotion existed, the kind that cuts you to the bone and nurses you back to health.

Her emotional landscape was like a child's drawing with lopsided proportions, nonsensical colors, and irregular borders. Nothing like the portrait of faithfulness before her.

It was beautiful and terrible, exalting and humbling to watch these sweet people navigate the final days of their long love affair.

When she did tear her gaze from the couple, she found Cole staring at her, his tender, steady, intense expression flayed her to her marrow.

She had no frame of reference for such powerful emotions. Her life consisted of browns and grays with some angry red thrown in for good measure. But Cole caused double rainbow shivers to race over her body. He radiated goodness and light.

She did not.

She handed the sick woman a throw from the nearby recliner. "Who wants cocoa?"

Mrs. McKillip's face lit up. "With whipped cream?"

"Absolutely," Jacey said and fled to the kitchen.

Once her hands stopped shaking, she meticulously put together the tray of cookies and cocoa, adding a dash of nutmeg to each cup and little sticks of peppermint to stir the hot chocolate. Strange how the simple act of serving people seemed to lower her blood pressure. Who knew she would enjoy it so much?

When she returned to the others, the scent of pine danced around her, and the room was dim except for the delicate illumination of the twinkle lights they'd expertly wrapped around the tree. Bing Crosby crooned *White Christmas* through the speakers and provided the perfect backdrop for the fairy fantasyland glow that engulfed the room.

Amazing. She'd walked into a Hallmark movie.

Her anxiety, distress and sadness slipped away with each step she took toward the tree and the people around it. She stood before them the most relaxed she'd been in days.

Moe trotted to her wearing a headband of reindeer antlers. "Moe-Moe, you're so festive. Who gave you those?" She set the tray on the coffee table and flicked the little bells that hung from the points.

"I gave them to him. They're what all the cool dogs are wearing." Cole grinned and her heart took a lap around her sternum.

He knelt next to a box of antique ornaments and handed them to the McKillips to hang on the tree.

Mr. McKillip helped his wife place a red and silver bell in the perfect spot. "Grab a bauble, little lady. This tree's not going to trim itself."

"As long as you help yourself to refreshments. This cocoa's not going to drink itself."

Mr. McKillip's big barrel laugh filled every corner of the room with joy. How did he manage it at such a tragic time? Bitterness simmered inside her on behalf of these people she barely knew.

She took a crystal snowflake from Cole and hung it next to a baby in a manger with King of the World written on it.

Tammy's earlier comment came back to her.

I figured if the King of the World loved me, warts and all...

That kind of love and acceptance was for other people, kind people, lovable people. Not her.

"Jacey, my dear, these cookies are as good as your Aunt Winnie's and I think this may be the best hot chocolate I've ever tasted," Mr. McKillip said.

"I agree." Mrs. McKillip yawned. "Oh, goodness, sorry. It's been an eventful day."

Mr. McKillip went to his wife and helped her stand. "Let's go to bed, before we turn into pumpkins."

Mrs. McKillip chuckled, then swayed on her feet.

Cole was at the wobbly woman's side in a flash. "Let me help you to your room. We can't have you crazy kids loitering around the halls all night." He winked at Mrs. McKillip.

A geyser of sorrow rose up in Jacey as she watched the three of them move towards the stairs. Cole held most of the small woman's weight as they made their way to the second floor. It wasn't fair. These were some of the nicest people she'd ever meet. They didn't deserve for a terrible disease to tear them apart.

Neither had her parents.

Her dad seemed so contrary now to everything hopeful, supportive, and real she saw in Cole and Mr. McKillip. Was her mother's suffering and death what turned his insides black? What would her life be like if her mother had lived? Or if she'd known Aunt Winnie...

She retreated to the kitchen to clean up. She could hear Cole near the tree when he came down as he tidied the room and put Winnie's ornament boxes in their rightful place. When he came to the kitchen to get water for the tree, she had to admit she was so glad to see him she nearly wept. The rest of her was irritated he continued to torture her. Why wouldn't he take the hint? There was nothing for him here.

"I think the tree looks good," he said and set the pitcher on the counter.

"Not bad," she agreed. "Thanks for the save."

"No problem. It was the fastest I've ever seen a tree decorated, but I think Mr. McKillip was trying to stay awake. He can blame it on his wife, but I saw him close his eyes when he hit the easy chair." He picked up a leftover cookie. "I heard four stitches and a goose egg for Maribeth. That's not too bad, huh?"

"Yes, I got a text from Tammy earlier. Glad that's all it was."

She wiped cocoa powder and sugar off the counter. *Go away, go away, go away... Don't make me look at you...*

"Anyway, I'm gonna head out but I want to give you something first." He stepped out the back door to retrieve something he'd obviously stashed on the porch. "This is for you," he said and handed her a beautifully wrapped gift.

"What's this for?"

"St. Patrick's Day."

Her head jerked up from inspecting the long rectangular package. "What?"

He laughed. "Kidding, Jacey. You know what it is. It's a Christmas gift."

She pushed the present back at him. "I... I didn't get you anything."

He pushed harder. "I didn't expect you to get me anything. I saw this and thought of you."

She should say no, but curiosity got the best of her. He already said he was leaving and she was sure he understood there could be no possible relationship. She wouldn't insult him further by rejecting his gift.

Curling ribbon circled her fingers as she carefully removed it from the package, slipped her finger under the tape, and slid the box free of the paper. Once the lid was off, her world tilted off its axis.

Nestled in pink polka dot tissue, a gorgeous doll peeked at her from under a mass of curly blonde hair. The crinkle of the paper and her heavy breathing were the only sounds in the kitchen as she lifted the baby. As she held it upright, soft blue eyes popped open and Jacey was in love.

"What is her name?" She tipped tissue on the floor and examined all sides of the box with her free hand. "The dolls my friends got usually had names. Does she have a name?"

"I don't know. I saw her at Ella's and thought of you. I know you said you didn't have a collection, but I thought you might want to start one. Winnie has a couple dolls up there."

"Here it is." Jacey studied the gold foil sticker. "Doll number 4658. Isabella…" She slumped into the chair, clutching the baby to her chest. He couldn't have known. There was no way he knew, yet he did. Of all the dolls in Ella's crowded shop, he found Isabella. And she could never, ever tell him that in all the years she wanted one and didn't get one, and in all the years the dolls went to other girls and not her, that she imagined one would someday be for her.

And she would name her Isabella.

Cole leaned to pet a sleeping Moe. "Is everything OK, Jacey? Do you not like the doll? You can trade her for whichever one you want."

"No, of course not, Cole. She's perfect."

And she was perfect, from her red sparkly velvet dress and crinoline underskirt to her black patent Mary Janes.

"OK, 'cause you look a little green and I can't tell if you're a happy shade of green or a get a bucket shade of green. I want you to be happy, Jacey. That's all I want."

The man devastated her. He'd gotten her a doll. The only thing she'd ever wanted. How had he known?

Her feet ached to run to him, her arms yearned to hold him, and *I love you* fought to escape her mouth.

She couldn't do any of those things. "I don't know what to say."

When he smiled, her heart finally gave up its valiant effort to remain steady and simply burst inside her chest.

"*Thank you* is usually customary."

And still, nothing came out of her mouth.

"Like I said, I'm gonna head home now, but I need you to do something with me in the morning. I'll pick you up early. There's someplace I need you to see."

She glanced at Isabella and nodded.

"Good. See you then."

"Cole," she said too loudly when she found her voice.

He stopped at the door. "Yes?"

"Thank you."

NINE

Cole relaxed in the quiet of Winnie's front porch and turned his good ear toward the mockingbird in the nearby sweet gum tree. No sound reached his ear when she fluttered her wings, and he heard no scrape or rustle with the brush of her body on the near bare branch. But with the pulse of her throat and the slight movement of her beak, a shrill song filled his head as did the answer from her companion close by.

Thank God I can still hear you...

"Cole? What are you doing out here?"

He stood and stuffed his hands into his sweatshirt pockets. "Waiting for you."

"You could've come in. Mr. McKillip is having coffee."

"I know. Are you ready?"

"Sure. Where are we going?"

"You'll see," he said and headed for the car.

The swish of their shoulder straps and the click of their seatbelts was in perfect rhythm like some weird synchronized vehicular dance. Everything else about them was painfully out of step as if they were two strangers in a car pool for the first time.

Jacey's hand brushed his when she moved to adjust the vent and he reached to put his phone on the charger. She jerked away. The gesture seemed wildly over-dramatic in the small space of the front seat, and served to further confirm what he had to admit.

She just wasn't interested. Not in him, not in the B&B, not in Cardinal Point.

"This won't take long." He pulled onto the two-lane road out of downtown. "I usually pass this place on my morning run. We could've jogged out here, but I know you're busy with the realtor today so…"

"Yeah, and I wanted to tell you I have the people from the church coming tomorrow to help me sort things and take what they want for their outreach ministries. If you want to be there for that, I think it'll take all day. I want to make sure you get what you want before I leave and the realtor takes over. And thanks for pulling the church people together. That's a big help."

Few things made Cole angry. He found it wasted energy and didn't change a thing, but Jacey Steele had managed to wake the well-controlled beast inside him.

How dare she sit there so smug and talk so flatly about walking out of his life? How dare she speak about Winnie's house with no sense of connection after she seemed to find some peace there? How dare she be nonchalant about the throngs of church people who would come with sad hearts and open arms to help her?

He whipped into the parking lot and hopped out as the car still settled into its spot. "This way," he said and slammed the door.

She scrambled behind him. "The church? Are we going to church today? It's the middle of the week."

He turned on her. "I wouldn't dream of bringing you to church, Jacey. That would be crazy. Crazy for you to actually visit the place that meant the most to Winnie and meet the people who were so anxious to know you and express their condolences. Why would you want to come here when you could get me to do your leg work and bring the church worker bees to you at the B&B to take Winnie's life apart?"

"I've only been here a short time, Cole. I haven't had a chan—"

"You've been invited, but it doesn't matter. You'll be gone soon. And as for me having what I want from the B&B, I already took the few things she mentioned over the years she wanted me to have. There was a quilt and some books, a few other things. I wanted her Bible, but I left it for you."

He stomped on, and she followed at his heels. "Take the Bible, Cole. I know it means something to you."

He flipped the latch on the aging steel gate to the church cemetery and stopped. "That's the problem. It should mean something to you."

"I can't help that I didn't know her and I can't change that overnight. I also can't help that I didn't have the same kind of religious life you shared with her. It's not the way I was raised."

"Completely not the point."

"Then what is the point, and why are you so angry with me all of a sudden?"

"I'm not angry. I'm irritated." He punched the metal sign that hung at the entrance. "OK, I'm angry." He dropped to a cement bench right inside the chain link fence that surrounded the church's graveyard. "Nobody cares about your career success or your lawsuit. Nobody here judges people based on their income or past mistakes. We try to co-exist and find peace and happiness and make a living. But you came in here so self-absorbed in your own mess, you didn't bother to embrace that and at least try to know Winnie before you sold her place for parts like an abandoned truck."

"That's not fair, Cole. You know I've struggled here to find pieces of my aunt, and I'm grieving for what I didn't know I lost. I'm sorry I am not what you wanted me to be. I tried and I don't fit."

"You fit, but you've scared yourself into believing you're three sizes too small for all the open, accepting space you've been given here."

She slumped beside him, deflated. "I don't know what you want me to say."

He left the bench and headed toward the well-worn path. "You know what? Forget about it. I'm sorry I started it."

She caught up to him and smoothed hair away from her face as she scanned the area. "Where are we going exactly?"

"To Winnie's grave. That's her church," he said and motioned beside them. "I suggest you visit there before you leave. It's a Texas Historic Landmark. Doors are open every day for visitors."

Cole trudged past familiar pecan trees and the hauntingly beautiful but hollow gazes of guardian angels perched on granite bases. Winnie's family plot came into view beneath the massive spread of an ancient live oak.

He stepped over the low black wrought iron fence that held the family in its well-kept rectangular patch of ground. It was both sad in its beauty and sacred in its quiet reverence to those who had helped settle Cardinal Point generations ago.

He offered his hand to her, but she'd already stepped inside and approached the fresh grave.

"There's no headstone yet," he said. "It takes time. Winnie had already picked something out. They'll call when they can come set it. The flowers from the funeral can stay there a while but then the caretaker will clear that away. Her friends are going to plant a rose bush or something when we get the headstone." He tried to read her expression but she was as blank as the aging markers where the names had been worn away. "I can leave you alone if you like. I thought you needed to see where your aunt is buried."

She stepped closer and then one knee seemed to give way before she slumped to the ground completely. "You don't have to leave. I'm going to sit here a minute."

He retreated to a bench in the corner. "Take as much time as you need."

Crunchy leaves skipped across brown winter grass and there was nothing from Jacey until she stood and slashed a tear from under her eye and stepped from plot to plot.

"These are Winnie and my mother's parents," she said and pointed.

"Yes. And their grandparents are over there. The ones with the flat markers."

"That's makes them my grandparents and great-grandparents, Cole. I didn't know they were here. I didn't know any of this. It's my whole history and I wasn't aware. How did they live? What did they look like?"

"I'm sure Winnie has lots of information at the house. Photo albums, keepsakes… There must be all kinds of information in her room somewhere. You'll find it."

Further over, she used her foot to move leaves and found a tiny, worn square. "This is a baby who died a hundred years ago."

Cole went to her side and picked a piece of dried grass from her sweater. "Yes. Lots of babies in an historic cemetery. You know the drill. No advanced medicine. Sometimes no doctor at all."

She nodded. "There are still spaces here. My mother should be here with her parents and her sister."

"Is she buried in Florida?"

"No. I was so little I don't remember much about it, but I don't think there was a funeral or anything. My dad had her cremated immediately. I've only recently remembered things he said when other people we knew died because of cancer. He never went to a memorial no matter how well we knew them and often made comments about what cancer did to a body. My dad has his faults, believe me, I know, but he didn't deserve to watch my mom die like that. It must have been horrible."

"In every way," he agreed. "I don't want to sound morbid or anything, but do you have her ashes? You could bring them here. Our pastor would probably help you come up with a small service or something. You could bury them here."

Color left her cheeks as her gaze moved from marker to marker. "I don't know. I really... don't know."

Cole touched her arm. "It's not important right this second. You can think about it later."

"What about your parents? They're here, too?"

"Yes," he said with his heart impaled on one of his ribs. "On the other side."

"Are we going to visit? I mean, we're here. If you don't mind me being with you."

He didn't mind. There were a million things he wanted to share with Jacey. His parents' graves fell on that list somewhere later. Like maybe after they'd confessed warm and fuzzy feelings for each other or she'd decided to come back to him after her issues in Florida were resolved.

Clearly, none of that was going to happen.

"No, I don't mind that you're with me. We can head that way. Do you need more time?"

"No. Thank you for bringing me here."

"You're welcome," he said and turned to move on.

Jacey sidled up beside him like a hungry kitten who wanted to follow him home. His fingers itched to take her hand and pull her closer to his side. The emotionally charged moments moved like waves crashing in and going out, and he felt perpetually confused by the motion. Did she want him to take her hand as she stuck to his side? Or would she reject him again?

He kept his hands to himself.

"Oh, look," she said and shielded her eyes from the sun to follow a bird as it flew across their path. "It's a red bird. The first one I've seen since I've been here. Ironic, since this place is called Cardinal Point." She paused to observe as the bright red male cardinal lit upon the fence around Winnie's plot and started his morning song. "Why is this place called Cardinal Point, anyway? There are no points here. There's barely a hill."

"Some people say it was an early settler who had family ties high up in the Catholic Church. Others say it was the Native Americans who lived here because the cardinal holds a place in their spiritual beliefs—as do most animals."

"Which do you believe?"

"Who knows? But there's a raging debate about it at most meetings of the historical preservation committee. Then there's the minority faction who believe it's based on one of the more widely known beliefs about the cardinal, but that one's tough to prove."

"Which belief is that?"

He laughed a little inside. This would be good. She was already freaked out about the heavy faith vibe surrounding Winnie's life, and he remembered how he reacted when he first heard the story. He believed Winnie got a sarcastic *yeah, right* as he hurried through the kitchen door with cookies in his mouth. Had to admit, though, there was a certain amount of comfort in the hardly believable notion. Especially since the cardinal visitor this morning seemed to want their attention as he remained on the fence and sang at the top of his lungs.

So, he decided to go for it. He'd already lost her romantically and there would be a huge humorous payoff he could share with his friends later when he would tell the story of how Jacey remembered she was surrounded by dead people and birds and made a high-speed exit from the cemetery.

"Some people believe cardinals represent loved ones who have passed on. They believe the birds show up when you need comfort or confirmation. They are a sign. A remembrance. They are your loved ones visiting you, checking in on you."

Jacey took a step back and looked from bird to him and back again. Several times. "Do you believe that?"

Boy, if they gave out little birdie Grammy Awards for the best vocal performance in a comedy/drama by a songbird, this fowl would have a mantle full of them for his escalating presentation.

"I believe if something makes you feel better or brings you peace, then why not? Winnie would say there are no coincidences. Sometimes you have you lose the logic and choose to believe."

"He's getting louder," she said with a hint of fear in her voice, "and he's changing his song. Why is he doing that? Why, Cole, *why*?"

Yeah, this was pretty hilarious, but also not very funny. She'd been through a lot, after all.

"OK, look up there." He put his arm around her stiffening shoulders. The scent of vanilla on her skin messed with his resolve as he bent to meet her nearly cheek-to-cheek so she could follow where he pointed. "Right there. He's talking to his mate.

Cardinals have all kinds of songs and strong family bonds. They talk differently to each other than they do their children, and there are different songs within those categories. Believe me, I spend a lot of time listening."

"I see her," she whispered and relaxed against him.

She seemed relieved to have spotted the rationale in the situation, but oddly disappointed the magic could be explained.

She stepped out of his reach. "How does that belief go with the name of the town? Seeing loved ones in red birds seems like more of a personal thing, don't you think?"

"Yes, but that story says there was a travelling doctor who said he was visited by more cardinals here than anywhere else on his route. The name grew from that. People who don't buy that theory say he was a drunken quack who hallucinated a lot of things."

Cole thought they were finished. He thought the cardinal discussion was over. He expected to move on.

But Jacey chose instead to return to the plot rather than run away. And the bird did his part when he didn't leave either. He simply changed his song.

"Cole? Do you think this is Aunt Winnie?"

"I don't know, Jacey. Do you?"

"No. I think it's my mother."

 C380

Jacey stood across the hall from the closed door of Winnie's bedroom, her thumb nail bitten to the quick, and Isabella in her arms. Moe sat sentinel at her feet. Cole's scathing accusation from earlier that she didn't care and hadn't tried to get to know her aunt reverberated through her brain.

He was right, of course. Her sparse knowledge of Winnie consisted of stories from him, the townspeople, and some ancient correspondence she'd accidentally stumbled upon while cleaning out a drawer.

Her father's betrayal was a dull knife to her soul, shredding and tearing its way to her core. How could he have been so heartless, then and now? Bubbles simmered in her stomach when she thought of their phone conversation... No, it hadn't been a conversation. He'd ranted against Winnie. His naked hostility toward a woman who was universally loved still mystified her because of his irrational reasoning. Responsible for her mother's death?

No.

Maybe there were more answers hiding beyond the closed door. Or not. What did it matter? The past was the past and she doubted any information she might glean from pilfering through a dead woman's things would change her life that dramatically. Besides, she'd been in Winnie's room... once... briefly, to nab a pair of earrings.

She must look like a childish idiot. A grown woman with a doll, cowering in the hall with her quasi guard dog. But the gift gave her comfort and Moe was her best friend, so, if she were doing this, she wasn't doing it alone.

Three fortifying breaths, two steps across the hall, one turn of the knob, and...

The scent of rose petals and *Beautiful* perfume swirled around her as she stepped into the room.

Tranquil light from gilded wall sconces and soft pink walls welcomed her into Winnie's haven.

Plush carpeting, the same color as the walls, caressed her socked feet and cushioned her steps as she made her way to the cozy window seat nestled in the crook of a huge bay window. The nook beckoned her to curl up and while away the day staring at the backyard garden. She lowered herself to the burgundy velvet cushions, her hands moving lazily over the soft fabric. As she surveyed the pretty room with its roses and ivy, a pang of longing to know the woman who'd created such a lovely, warm space latched onto her.

Had Winnie read to her while sitting on this comfy bench? Or let her play with the colorful bottles of perfume and fluffy powder puffs lined up across the top of the antique vanity next to the window?

Unable to resist, she went to the dressing table to investigate all the treasures it held. A round blue box with a clear lid caught her eye. A puff with a white bow rested inside. It tickled her nose and made her sneeze when she inhaled the loose scented powder. Smiling, she glanced in the mirror and wiped the white smudge from the tip of her nose.

In the middle of the room stood a four-poster bed with downy white bedding like the meringue on a coconut cream pie. It was the kind of bed you snuggled in, jumped on, and dreamed of Prince Charming in, the perfect place for a beloved aunt to cuddle her niece and tell her fairytales.

The pang of longing came again, but this time, it carried melancholy on its back. This charming room represented every loving thing she'd missed as a child.

According to her father, disappointment was a wasted emotion. His voice plowed through her head again. *You don't like something? Fix it. If you can't fix it, get over it.*

Determined to *get over it*, she retrieved Isabella from the window seat and set her on the bedside table next to Winnie's glasses, a pink tube of hand cream and a box of tissues. The most prominent item there was Winnie's large black Bible. This wasn't a Family Bible that sat unopened on a coffee table. The cracked cover and taped spine held well-worn pages that crinkled when she flipped through it. The contents had been underlined, highlighted and dog-eared from years of obvious daily use. This book was important to her aunt. It was a connection to a God who wasn't just written on plaques around her home. He was as real to Winnie as Moe was to her. She didn't understand that kind of relationship, but she could respect it.

She gently set the Bible next to Isabella.

A Victorian lamp sat on a white crocheted doily nearby. She stroked the pink fringe dangling from the shade and studied the painting above Winnie's bed. A field of bluebonnets stretched out in front of a small, rundown farmhouse. The flowers blew in the breeze as the last rays of daylight shone behind the house. The artist perfectly captured the disparity between the crude man-made structure and the glory of the surrounding nature. On impulse, she grabbed the frame and removed it from the wall. This would go to Florida with her.

A group of photos on a round cherry wood table caught her eye. She approached the pictures as if they were a ticking bomb. She braced herself for another explosion of discovery.

A gasp raced past her vocal chords when her gaze landed on the first image. A gorgeous, blonde bride beamed from under the brim of an eighties-era veiled hat. Her big hair curled around her shoulders and down her back. Billowing puffed sleeves tried but could not hide her happily-ever-after smile.

The groom's chestnut hair winged away from his handsome, jubilant face and brushed the collar of his slate tuxedo jacket. The gray and black tie and dove gray vest accentuated the stunning ring on her perfectly manicured hand as it rested on his satin lapel. The orange sherbet carnation in his boutonniere set off the blue in their sparkling eyes.

She'd never seen a picture of her parents together. Happiness radiated from their faces at the start of their life together, but she'd never known for sure since her father had never shared an image like this. Why? It could have only brought her peace.

She traced their faces with her finger. The details of the photo, especially the over-the-moon-happiness of her father, would not fit into her head. She'd never, ever, seen that look on his face. So foreign, she couldn't believe the man who raised her could even arrange his face into an expression so joyful.

Sadness and self-pity consumed her. She'd been robbed. She'd grown up without a mother and without this man as a father. The neglected little girl inside of her wailed *unfair, unfair, unfair ...*

Was it her? Or was he incapable of love? The photo answered that question. He was capable of loving someone, but not her. The desolate reality plowed into her.

I've been unlovable since I was born.

The next snapshot of a young Winnie and her mother teased a smile from her deep sadness. The sisters were laughing and holding an uncooked turkey by each of its plump legs. It was the kind of picture you would smile at whether you knew the people or not.

There were a few of her when she was very little, one in a swim suit with a water hose, another of her and a big collie dog. She gathered them all and put them on the bed to box up and take to Florida.

Elbow macaroni covered the frame around the last photo she lifted from its dusty spot. Touched by time, pieces had long since chipped away or fallen off, and Jacey realized she held her own pre-school artwork in her hands. In this most precious picture of all, her little arms wrapped around her mother's neck, their foreheads and noses touched. Their eyes were closed, and the light filtering through the trees created a halo around them. Her blonde hair, held away from her face with a ladybug headband, stood out in stark contrast to her mother's bald head with its patches of baby-fine fuzz that glistened in the setting sun.

Painful in its beauty. Healing in its pain. As comforting as a lullaby.

The image of mother and daughter pacified the squalling child inside her, her only wish to crawl into the photo and curl into her mother's arms, a living breathing thing.

Moe bumped her leg with his nose and continued to press until she was forced to look away. "I don't think I've ever appreciated you more than today, pooch." She scooped him into her arms. His warm presence soothed the final tremors from the hail storm of feelings she'd just endured. "Thanks for not letting me stand here with this picture indefinitely."

She set the photo with the rest of the *take to Florida* pile and added Winnie's personalized jewelry box and a book about the history of Cardinal Point that included a section about the B&B.

The simple act of sorting helped her regain her equilibrium. She stood near the bed feeling a little more like herself as Moe continued to keep her on task.

"Check it out," she said when she discovered a VCR on a shelf below the old TV. "Are you up for a movie tonight?"

The cabinet with the tapes held a variety of titles from *Beauty and the Beast* to *Butch Cassidy and the Sundance Kid* to *It's a Wonderful Life*. There were also sermons and Bible studies. Stacked on the bottom were a few home movies, *Founders Day Celebration, Christmas Pageant 1988, Cole's Eagle Scout Award Ceremony*, but none of those mattered once she saw the one entitled *Jacey and Leah*.

Her insides quaked. The shiver caused her hand to shake so hard she tore the sleeve as she grappled to free the VHS from its cardboard prison. A slide, a click and it was in the slot. Her sweaty hands fumbled with the controls on the TV. An attempt with the remote was hardly better, but she finally found the correct buttons.

Static made its way to a patch of grass as someone wrestled with the camcorder and a woman gave instructions off camera. Then female laughter. Abruptly, the front of the B&B came into focus. The camera panned to show the front yard and her mother sitting in a lawn chair. Her scarfed head tilted back, her face to the sun.

"Smile, Leah," a woman said.

Leah turned to the camera, her hollow cheeks, and tired, sunken eyes clearly visible. But her smile was brilliant. "Don't film me, Winnie. Film the Amazing Jacey," she said and swept her hand out in the direction of the yard.

The camera panned to her three-year-old self in a sleeveless, yellow terry cloth short suit and a pink cape. Her little muscular arms glistened with sweat and her blonde ponytail blew in the wind.

"Show us what you've got, Amazing Jacey," Winnie said.

She danced, then ran, her cape flapping behind her. "Watch this, Mommy. Mommy. Watch me."

There was laughter from the women. "I'm watching you, love. Aunt Winnie and I can't wait to see what you can do now."

Pre-schooler Jacey put one leg in front of the other and raised her hands, then turned to the camera. "Are you watching?"

"Yes," The two women said in unison.

She then performed three perfect cartwheels in a row and then stood with her fists on her hips. "Ta-da! Philippians four. I can do all thing through Christ who strengthens me."

There was whooping and clapping from off camera.

She blew kisses and ran to her mother. "Did you see? Did you see, Mommy?"

"I saw you, my strong girl."

"Aren't you proud of me?"

"Yes. Very proud." Her mother smoothed a stray piece of hair from Jacey's face.

"Aren't you glad I'm your daughter and I can turn three cartwheels?"

Her mother laughed and lifted Jacey into her lap. "Jacey, I want you to listen to me." Leah's tone turned very serious. "If you lined up all the little girls in the whole wide world and told me to pick one to be my daughter. I. Would pick. You. Not because you can turn a cartwheel, but because you're you. My girl, who I love more than my own life." Then she kissed Jacey's nose. "I love you, Amazing Jacey because you're Jacey and you're amazing, just the way you are."

"And I would pick you out of all the mommies in the world because you make the bestest pancakes." She jumped off her lap and ran out of the frame.

The camera stayed on her mother.

"Do you think she'll remember me and how very much I love her?" Leah asked, never taking her eyes from her daughter.

There was sniffing and the camera shook a little. "I'll make sure she remembers. I'll tell her every chance I get," Winnie said from behind the lens.

Tears rolled down Leah's cheeks and she nodded.

Then the static returned.

An inhuman wail shattered the silence. Heartache rose, surged and engulfed her body. Like a bayou breaking its bank, she was helpless to stop the deluge of grief. She clung to the memory of her mother's tortured face. She'd been loved and loved deeply. So much so that her mother's dying wish had been for her to remember she was special and wanted.

She held the macaroni frame, the image now told a more profound story. Love flowed between the two of them like a visible current. A portrait of a child basking in her mother's adoration, a mother desperate to convey everything she felt in the time she had left.

A prayer.

A benediction.

For the most precious person in her life, her daughter.

Another sob wracked her body. She held herself around her middle to hold the pieces together, but they blew apart, jumbled up, and rearranged themselves. She crawled onto the bed, curled her body around Isabella, and gave into the tears. Her mother's words, the last thing she heard before sleep took her.

I.

Would pick.

You.

TEN

"I cannot believe I let you talk me into wearing this." Jacey marched behind her gymnasts in the Christmas parade, sporting a red sweatshirt with CP GYMNASTICS spelled out in sparkling crystals.

"Frankly, I can't either." Tammy waved and flirted with the crowd. She wore the maternity version of Jacey's top. "I thought you'd fight me tooth and nail."

"It was thoughtful of you to torture... I mean include Moe as well." The dog pranced at the end of his leash in his own tricked out CP GYMNASTICS shirt.

"You both look awesome." Tammy blew kisses to a group of senior citizens congregated at the corner of McKinney and First Street. "You can never have too much bling in your life. Since I made them for the whole team, I couldn't possibly leave you and Moe out of the fun."

Jacey's inexperienced laughter stumbled from her mouth. She still wasn't used to finding so many things laugh-out-loud funny. She and Moe in matching shirts that rivaled most marquis light displays was one of those moments. In the past, it would have left her mortified. "You're right," she conceded. "We look awesome."

Tammy cut her a sidelong glance. "What's gotten into you?"

"What do you mean?"

"That monster size chip on your shoulder seems to have shrunk significantly."

"Hey, I don't have a chip on my shoulder."

Tammy rolled her eyes. "OK, boulder. We both know it's a boulder."

Jacey tried not to laugh again. "I'll admit to a chip."

The parade stopped for the Cardinal Point High School dance team to perform a routine while the band played their rendition of *Here Comes Santa Claus*. As the trumpet line honked out a solo, the gymnasts did an impromptu dance of their own. It was a lot less coordinated and quite a bit sillier than the Red Bird Dancers who'd taken district, regional, and area top honors three years in a row. She knew this because at least six near strangers had told her so.

Tammy bumped her shoulder. "So?"

"So what?"

"What's changed?" Tammy wiggled her eyebrows. "It's Cole, isn't it? He's been kissin' you senseless with those big ol' luscious lips of his, hasn't he? Melted that boulder right down to a pebble, huh? "

"Yes, Cole." She bent to straighten Moe's shirt. "But also you, and the McKillips, and this town, and the cemetery, and the B&B. It's everything. You know, I went through Winnie's room and found answers to some questions that have plagued me my whole life. They were sitting there in plain sight for me to see and hold and experience. I can't even explain the roller coaster ride I've been on since I came here."

"No matter how rough the ride's been, you've managed to hold on."

If Tammy only knew how tenuous the thread was that kept her tethered to the track. She'd been thrown out, tossed on the rails, and hurled off the side in the dark tunnels. Yeah, she was still holding on, but her feelings and reactions were all over the map. She loved Cole but couldn't keep him. Her father's betrayal made her doubt every moment of her life. The love of her mother and aunt now crept in to save her from her apparent destiny to remain untouchable, unreachable, and unlovable.

Still, she couldn't take the chance.

"Heads up, girls!" She clapped. "Time to move. And smile!"

Tammy didn't let her get far. "Uncovering secrets can be a good thing, Jacey. Isn't that what you wanted here? To find the truth?"

"Yes. In a way, I guess. But the truth is hard. Even the good truth. I've always believed there was something innately wrong with me. My mother died and left me, my father held me at arm's length and had me convinced I wasn't good enough for anything. What I found in Winnie's room changed that. There were pictures, videos… It was obvious my mother and Winnie loved me very much. Those images started a healing inside of me that I thought impossible. And it's too big to even grasp. It's good, but it's staggering. It's brought me peace, but I'm not whole yet. I don't know if I'll ever be."

Tears swam in Tammy's eyes.

Panic froze Jacey's limbs. "Oh, no. Don't you dare cry, Tammy. If you start, then so will I."

The other woman fanned her face with her hands and sniffled a little. "All right. I'm fine." She fanned harder. "I'm fine. That's so great. I'm really happy for you." Her pudgy arm went around Jacey's shoulders for a brief side hug.

She shocked herself by snaking her arm around Tammy's waist and squeezing. "Thanks, Tammy. For everything."

"I have to admit I was hoping you'd finally decided to stay in Cardinal Point and give your relationship with Cole a chance." Tammy released her and surreptitiously wiped her eyes.

"You know I can't do that. I'm leaving as soon as the parade's over. The McKillips checked out. The house is in the hands of Cole and the realtor. I have to go. I refuse to drag Cole into the mess that is my life."

"And you know I think you're crazy, right?"

"You've made that perfectly clear." She tried to smile at her pregnant friend, but no matter how hard she tried she couldn't get the corners of her mouth to curl the right direction.

"But seriously, Jacey, I think he really—"

"Tammy, in the last two months, I've had an athlete seriously injured, lost my job, and been sued. Then, I find out about an aunt I never knew I had, and discovered a horrible betrayal by my father. Not to mention the recent revelations about my mother. During all this, I met an amazing man who I've had to admit deserves someone much better than me. It hurts like crazy, but I can't stay here for Cole. It's not fair to him."

"Shouldn't you let Cole decide what's fair and not fair to him? He has a say in this, doesn't he? Have you really talked to him about how you feel and what God's best might be for the both of you?"

Jacey winced at the too-true words. In all honesty, she hadn't let him say much. And though she'd begun to scratch the surface of a relationship with God, she was in no way qualified to determine His best for herself or anyone. "He knows I'm leaving. There's not much else to say at this point." She took Tammy's hand. "I want you to know, the best part of my journey here is that I've found my first real girlfriend. I have a ton of baggage to sort through and a lot to process. Thank you for being here for me. I'm better, but who knows how long it'll be until I can function like a normal human being?"

A giant tear ran down Tammy's cheek. "Well, now you've done it. You can't say stuff like that to a pregnant woman and expect her not to cry." She looped her arm through Jacey's. "And, for the record, normal is overrated."

The parade made its way into the center of Cardinal Point where the crowds doubled. The picturesque square looked as charming as it had the first day she'd rolled into town. She could barely fit the events of the last month into her brain. In some ways her life was completely different. In others, it was exactly the same.

The festive happiness and good cheer of the residents seeped into her pores and mixed with her blood, binding her to them with a shared small-town-pride strand of DNA. With that video, she knew she'd been here before. Cardinal Point was her town, too, because it belonged to her mother and Winnie, and all her family before.

She breathed in the aroma of fresh roasted coffee beans from Songbird's Bakery and the scent of freshly cut pine from the trees that lined the square. That, and the massive amount of hair spray Tammy had spritzed on the girls mingled with the trace of manure from the horses at the back of the group. From now on, this bouquet of smells would always remind her of Cardinal Point.

A thrill skittered up her back when she passed Cole as he stood next to a barricade that sequestered spectators. His hesitant smile and small wave shredded her soul like a love note ripped into a million pieces.

"Are you sure?" Tammy's voice could barely be heard over the masses.

For a second, she nearly lost her resolve, but she loved him too much to subject him to her drama. And truth be told, she was afraid. Afraid she couldn't handle a real, mature relationship. She knew she stood in her own way, but had no idea how to push herself out of her own path. It could take a while to shake the impact of her father's duplicity. Who knew how bad it would get before it got better?

Cole didn't deserve to witness the total collapse.

She and Tammy corralled their team out of the parade line and gathered them in front of the courthouse where the dads pulled out mats. Her nerves crackled with anticipation as the girls prepared to perform their demonstration.

Jacey clapped to get their attention. "OK, ladies, listen up. This is it. Your grand finale. You'll start at this end. When you get to the other side, circle around and get back in line." Their little anxious faces tugged on her heartstrings. "You don't have to be perfect. All we ask is that you do your best. But most of all, I want you to have tons of fun. Can you do that for me?"

A chorus of *Yes, Miss Jacey* made her smile.

"OK, then. Show them what you've got. And remember, have fun."

They whooped and hollered as they lined up, and Tammy motioned for the event coordinator to start the music.

With every leap, back walkover, front walkover, and flip they executed, confidence unfurled in each girl like a flag over a proud country.

And she was reminded why she loved gymnastics so much.

They ended with handstands, performed with perfect technique. The longer they stayed with their feet in the air, the louder the audience applauded. The expressions of triumph and pride on the girls faces matched the gratification that swirled, swelled and spread through every cell of Jacey's body.

"They did it." Tammy wrapped Jacey in a hug.

Jacey laughed and returned the embrace. "Yes, they did."

They were nearly knocked to the ground when the whole team swarmed, giving high fives and bear hugs to both coaches.

"You guys were awesome. I couldn't be prouder." Her face hurt from smiling so much.

Tammy did a little jig. "Best gymnastics exhibition I've ever seen."

One by one, the girls peeled away from the group and into their parents' arms to continue the day of celebration on the square.

"Thank you, Miss Jacey. See you after Christmas break," one of them said as she disappeared into the mass of people.

Jacey couldn't bear to call out that she wouldn't be there.

Tammy herded her own kids into a circle to say good-bye, her wet cheek pressing against Jacey's in a final hug. "Be careful. I hope everything gets better in Florida. Keep me posted."

Her rib cage sagged as she melted into her friend's embrace. "I will."

Tammy pulled a tissue from her sleeve and wiped her eyes. "I hope you find what you're looking for, Jacey, and remember, Jesus loves you, and so do I."

Tammy took her hand for a final squeeze.

Then her only friend slipped out of her grasp and into the crowd.

∞

Jacey set another box by the door. "Give me another minute, Moe. Then we'll be on our way."

For someone who didn't want anything and wasn't interested in most of Winnie's odd décor, she sure had a carload of stuff to take back to Florida. Still, after days of donating, cleaning, and giving things to Winnie's friends, there seemed to be a house full of items left to deal with. The church said they'd have a yard sale for charity after the place sold, and Cole was going to list some things on surrounding community Facebook pages. Surely someone needed the wicker patio furniture from the back yard and the collection of state plates Winnie had nailed to one whole wall in the formal dining room.

There were likely hidden treasures amongst the obvious Victorian reproductions scattered throughout the house. Maybe someone else would strike gold with a real antique. For Jacey, all the gold she needed came by way of Winnie's personal items—especially the pictures and videos. She'd even packed the VCR so she was sure she could view the tape again and again until she had it converted to a DVD.

As for the Bible, she left it for Cole. She'd text him it was there as soon as she cleared the city limits.

"I guess that's it," she said to the dog.

She made one more pass by every side door to make sure they were locked. Mockingbirds and wrens fluttered by the near empty feeder off the porch. She'd been looking for cardinals ever since she'd been lured by the legend Cole told her in the cemetery. That day, she was sure she'd had a visitor. Now the whole idea seemed far away and silly.

"Yeah," she mumbled to herself, "silly. So silly you're wishing it would happen again."

A minivan pulled into the drive as she prepared to leave. One of her gymnasts jumped out with an oversized gift bag.

"Miss Jacey. I missed you after the parade."

"Carly? What's up?"

"This is for you. It's a Christmas and thank you present."

Jacey took the bag and struggled to coax a simple response from between her dry lips.

"Look inside," Carly said.

Jacey set the bag on the porch step and pulled out a large Mason jar with a lopsided bow on the side.

"It's cookies in a jar," Carly said and puffed out her little chest. "Made it myself. All you have to do is add the eggs and butter. See? I wrote the directions on the tag."

Jacey studied the layers of white and brown sugar, flour, and chocolate chips. "It's perfect, Carly, and you did such a good job." She fought to keep an emotional quiver out of her voice. She couldn't remember the last time any of her students truly remembered her during the holidays. "I've been doing a lot of baking lately. I can't wait to try your recipe."

"My mom put something else in the bag, too, but this is the good stuff."

Jacey laughed and accepted the girl's tight hug. "Thank you."

Carly's mom leaned out the window. "Glad we caught you. Thought maybe you'd gone to the hospital."

"Hospital? Wh... Why would I go to the hospital?"

"I'm sorry. Thought you knew. There was an accident not too long after the parade. A car tried to go around one of the barricades that had been set up along the parade route."

Faces of all the people she knew and loved in Cardinal Point flashed through her mind. Tammy, her kids... *Cole*... "You said hospital. Where there injuries?"

"My husband said they took one person out by ambulance."

Jacey stumbled. "Do you know who?"

Carly hopped in the van. "I know who."

"Tell me."

"Mr. Boudreaux."

ELEVEN

Cole dropped his phone in his pocket and pulled his chair closer to the hospital bed. "Don't try to get up, Grandpa."

"I have to go to the bathroom." He rattled the side rail. "And I need something to drink."

"The nurse is going to help you with a bed pan."

Grandpa tossed the blanket aside. "No, sir."

"Yes, sir. And you can't drink anything in case you need surgery. We're waiting on x-rays and they're probably going to do a CT scan or an ultrasound to make sure there's no internal bleeding."

"I don't need surgery, boy. I need to go home. All I need's a Band-Aid for this scratch on my arm."

Cole studied the 'scratch'. Liquid oozed from the massive purple, black, and bloody scrape on his Grandpa's arm. There were probably more like it on his torso and thigh. The staff had only begun to wrestle him out of his clothes for evaluation. He'd still be on the back board if the old man hadn't ripped off the collar and rolled free.

"Grandpa, please. They'll sedate you if you don't cooperate. You were hit by a car. They have to assess the damage."

"I was tapped by a car, boy, and I bounced right off the concrete. I'm fine."

"Yeah, you bounced, all right. You bounced a couple of times."

The stubborn man sat back in the bed with a sigh that sounded like deep slicing pain. Cole's gut twisted with concern. Where was that doctor? "I'm going to stick my head out and see what's happening. I'm also going to tell the state trooper to come back later for your statement." He paused at the curtain. "Stay in that bed."

Grandpa clutched the edge of the sheet and closed his eyes. Whether his parting grunt was a yes or a no, Cole didn't know, but he knew he couldn't leave him for long.

Medical personnel darted back and forth in the narrow hall, and worried family members tended to their loved ones behind flimsy curtains. Mercifully, Grandpa was the only injury from the debacle at the parade, but the regional hospital's ER was overrun with sick kids and chest pains. He tried to rub the knot out of the back of his neck as he searched for their nurse, but it was hard to keep his mind on the mission. Images of Grandpa's frail body on the ground rolled through his head over and over, and the obligatory chorus of *if onlys* played on and on in his ears. *If only he'd been on the other side of the street, if only he'd seen the car sooner, if only the idiot kid behind the wheel had followed the rules.*

If only he hadn't been so preoccupied with Jacey's departure...

"Are you looking for us?" The sweet nurse and two others approached the small room, supplies in hand. "Since he's stable, the doctor put in orders. We're going to get started on bloodwork and get him downstairs for some tests."

Cole smirked. Grandpa was going to love all that. "I'll give you a hand with him," he said. "He really needs to get to the bathroom."

She held up a package Cole recognized as a catheter. "We'll take care of it."

"Like I said, I'll give you a hand." He smiled. "It's really more for your protection."

"Not necessary," she said and bustled right past him. "He's not our first grumpy old guy of the day. We'll take good care of him."

"I know, but—"

"No worries, hon. You should head to the lounge for coffee or go get some food before the cafeteria closes. He's not going anywhere soon. With his age and the nature of the accident, he'll probably be admitted."

Admitted? It never occurred to him Grandpa wouldn't be at home in his recliner at six o-clock to watch the news. Especially on a day he would actually be the news. It wasn't that he didn't know he was hurt, he knew it could be a lot worse than he suspected. But this was big, strong, Grandpa—the only family he had. The closest person he had left in the world.

His phone vibrated in his pocket. It'd blown up after the accident so he'd put it on silent. Now Shane texted he was on his way, and strangers who'd come all the way from the news station in Austin wanted to talk to him.

He poked his head into the room where his cantankerous grandfather seemed to melt beneath the soft, smiling words of the pretty redhead who took his blood. At least he wasn't still trying to bolt from the bed. "I'm right out here if you need me, Grandpa."

Noise surrounded him. Beeping machines, rumbling voices, and rolling carts made little sense when jumbled together in his bad ears.

But one voice seemed to find him in the fog after a particularly loud crash.

"Cole! Cole!"

"Jacey?"

She barreled down the hall like in some television medical drama. A spinning bed stand banged against the wall in her wake as the tray it held slid across the tile floor and into another room.

"Thank God you're all right." She crashed against him so hard he stumbled back. For someone who seemed so concerned about his well-being, she sure was trying to break a rib.

He grabbed her upper arms to set her away. "Of course I'm all right. Why wouldn't I be?"

She jabbed at his abdomen and even smashed her hand into his face as if checking for something. He couldn't imagine what. Last time he checked in the mirror, all the basic stuff was still in the right place.

She stood back and then suddenly bent to catch her breath. "Carly," she gasped with her hands on her knees, "Carly said you were hurt." She pulled herself upright. "Aw, man, I ran too fast."

He hated that he was glad to see her, and hated that she seemed genuinely concerned about him. Hadn't she tortured him enough? "What are you doing here, Jacey? I thought you were on the road to Florida."

"I told you. Parade, car, ambulance… Are you sure you're OK?"

"I'm fine. It was Grandpa who was injured."

She clutched his arm and went pale. "Oh, no. Is he OK?"

"He will be."

"What happened?"

"Some kid got antsy in the traffic. Thought he could drive around the cones. Pulled right out where people were still walking from the parade. Then he second-guessed his stupidity and decided to back up into Grandpa, who wouldn't even had been there if he wasn't coming to meet me."

"I'm so sorry, Cole. What are his injuries?"

"He's banged up. They're checking everything. He's so old and frail they're sure he broke something, but they don't know what."

"Is he in a lot of pain?"

"Not that he'll admit. They're running tests and trying to make him comfortable."

"What can I do?"

"Nothing, Jacey. He's in good hands. Thanks for coming by." Nothing felt better in that moment than turning to walk away. He didn't have time to nurse her poor self-esteem or tell her she was beautiful or pursue their new relationship. He'd gotten nowhere on that path before she'd shut it down, and he was in no mood to slip his heart under her knife and let her stab at it again. Enough. "I'll text you when we get an offer on the B&B."

"Cole, wait. Let me help."

Was she serious? What could she possibly do to help? Right now, all he wanted to do was find a hot cup of coffee and a quiet corner and contemplate the truth that Grandpa wasn't going to live forever. Then he'd hit the hospital chapel and pray to God he'd have him a while longer because, quite frankly, he was tired of losing people.

"Cole, stop!"

He turned on her at the door to the stairwell. "What do you want, Jacey?"

"I told you, I was worried about you. I thought you were hurt. I want to help."

"Go on back to Florida. I got this."

This time, when he turned, she clawed at his coat like a three-year-old ready to pitch an all-out hissy fit. "Cole, please—"

"Please what?" He yanked away and leaned against the door. "Look around you, Jacey. This is real life. This is where people are born and where people come to die. This isn't the tiny little world of your gym where you show up, do your thing, and boss people around. You can't perform here. You can't blame everything on your horrible father here. This is the real stuff. The tough stuff. It isn't about you, and you should only be here for me if you're all in. And you're not all in. You made that clear."

He should have never looked into her eyes. There was terror there tangled up with confusion. He'd hurt her feelings. Good. She didn't belong there because she'd made her choice. But he was still crazy about her and she was still an emotional mess of a woman who was trying to find her way. He'd plain run out of time and energy for all her soul-searching at his expense.

Her keys rattled in her pocket as she fished to retrieve them. "I'm sorry I bothered you." She met his steady gaze. "Give your grandfather my best," she said on a heavy breath as though she'd taken a punch to the gut.

Regret picked at his resolve. "Look, I appreciate your concern. Thank you…"

But she'd already walked away and he didn't know which was harder: watching her really leave, or knowing she wouldn't stay for him.

He burst into the stairwell. Metal met beige cinder block as the door crashed against the wall and he tried to escape downstairs.

When he hit the fifth step, a flash of lucidity penetrated his brain. Why had she come? *How* had she come? The place was crawling with state police and reporters who'd come to get the real story on the driver and his victim. Hospital security was on high alert to keep the right people in and the curiosity seekers out. Yet, Jacey had found the hospital and a place to park in record time.

And she found him, looking like she'd run all the way.

He grabbed the rail and propelled himself back up the stairs. She appeared to be long gone until he hit the ER exit. Just past the patient drop-off circle and a few yards from the Channel 24 news van, he spotted her and her overloaded sensible car.

Angus, an officer from the Cardinal Point PD, was giving her grief for the way she'd left it in a no parking zone—and with one tire on the sidewalk.

"I got it, Angus. She's a friend of the family."

The burly officer didn't seem to like it, but he grunted and moved on.

"Oh," she huffed, "so now I'm a friend of the family?" She marched to the driver's side.

He tapped on the roof. "C'mon, move this over there. I need to talk to you."

"This place is a mad house. There's nowhere to park. That's how I ended up here in the first place."

"I can see that, but can you at least roll it off the sidewalk? The last thing we need is two traffic mishaps in one day."

He was being completely logical. She, however, hitched her chin in such a way that he knew she was about to speed off the same way she came and would probably run over his foot in the process.

He snatched the keys out of her hand before she could slip inside.

"I'll do it," he said. "Hop in."

"No, thanks."

"Fine. I'll meet you right over there."

She raced to the end of the row where he stopped, and hovered near the door as he got out. "Thank you," she said and held out her hand for the keys.

He kept them. "Why did you come here, Jacey?"

"I told you, I was worried. I thought you were hurt."

"You could've called Tammy. She knows everything. You were on your way out of town."

"So what? I was concerned. Carly said they took Mr. Boudreaux to the hospital. I thought it was you because I've heard the kids call you that. I was scared and I…"

"Exactly."

"Exactly what?"

"Ok," he said. "I don't have time for this, so I'm gonna spell it all out for you. You have feelings for me, Jacey. Real feelings. And I think you know I have strong feelings for you, too. It scares you and I get that. But it scared you more to think something happened to me. You thought I was in trouble. You dropped everything and flew over here like a mama bear. Like someone who loves someone and is scared half to death they might lose them."

"That's not what happened."

"The sidewalk begs to differ. Where's Moe?"

Her seizure-like gasp was almost comical. "Omigosh, Moe!"

"Where is he?"

"He better be sitting on Winnie's porch. I left so fast… I think I asked Carly to toss him in the house. I need to go."

"No, you're not going anywhere until we settle this."

"There's nothing to settle, Cole. My home, my job… Everything is in Florida. I have a mess there, I told you that. I have to clean it up."

"Not really. That mess will still be there after Christmas. You do realize Christmas is in two days, don't you? Tomorrow is Christmas Eve."

"I'd forgotten…"

"You really forgot when Christmas is after all we went through with the McKillips and the parade today? It's worse than I thought. You only want to run to Florida because you have more control there than you do here. You'd rather be in that mess alone on Christmas where you know it's a disaster than here with me where you might be happy. And what happens after your career crisis is over? The same life? The same misery? The same daddy issues?"

"It's not that simple."

"Sure it is and, once again, my grandpa needs me, so I'll clear it up. You, Jacey Steele, are a coward. A real live, yellow-bellied coward. Your problem is not with me or falling in love. Your problem is you. Your biggest issue is your father. He did a terrible thing and continued to do it for years. And what do you do instead of confront him? You run away from everything and let him win. He kept you down, but you're willing to stay down. When are you going to get up, Jacey? When are you going to take back your life?"

No response.

"Fine. I'm done. Send me a postcard and a bag of oranges from The Sunshine State."

This is where he should have stalked off.

But he didn't.

He scooped her into his arms and kissed her instead. It wasn't all that smooth or pretty, but he didn't have time to finesse his moves. She didn't exactly fight him off, but she didn't exactly kiss him back either.

At first.

Then she appeared to be all in.

He set her away from him. "Yeah, right. You don't love me." He grabbed her hand and dropped her keys into her palm. "And I don't love you, either."

TWELVE

Jacey hit the gas and sped past a large paneled truck. Moe whimpered in the back seat and made sure his head was in the center of her rearview mirror as he walked atop the boxes and bags in the back seat. Early winter darkness had already overtaken the skies. Moe's shadowy figure in the headlights behind her didn't help anything.

"You gotta lie down, pooch. I can't see through your furry head."

The dog decided to move into the front seat instead. He used her right shoulder as a place to steady himself as he moved around the loaded car like a chess piece. He landed in the passenger seat with a thud and whimpered again.

"I know you need out. I'm trying to get to Exit 121. That's where the big Louisiana welcome center is. We can hang out there for a while."

Back in the right lane, she mindlessly poked at the buttons on the radio. Selections alternated between Cajun Christmas carols and static until a massive headache blocked out all interest in music.

Moe's whimper turned to an outright yip and cry, and something about his pained little face was the final pebble on the scale that tipped her into hysteria.

"Who am I kidding?" she wailed.

Every worn out joint in her body protested the long drive. Her left arm tingled for a while then went totally numb from her death-grip on the wheel. Her recent penchant to go on crying jags, after years of not crying at all, once again blurred her vision and turned her into a blubbering heap.

Cole was right. Right about everything. She was a huge, feather-brained chicken.

A huge, unhappy, cry-baby, feather-brained chicken.

A huge, unhappy, emotionally stunted, cry-baby, feather-brained chicken.

She passed another sign for the Atchafalaya Welcome Center. "Won't be long now, pooch. Then we'll figure out what to do."

But what was she going to do? And how was she going to do it?

Everything about her was in misery. There was no peace or happiness about leaving Cardinal Point. She stupidly thought there would be. She truly thought going home to Florida was the right call, that there'd be some sort of quiet calm overtake her as she headed back to face her problems. But, no. Every mile—every inch—she moved farther from Cole and the B&B felt like a long walk into a dark, dank, and distorted black hole.

"This can't be right, Moe. I don't want to die in a black hole in Florida."

Moe had given up. He lay on his side, vacantly staring at the heating vent. He didn't want to die in her tiny apartment in Florida, either. He wanted the wide-open space of Winnie's wraparound porch, and the doggie treats every store owner on the square gladly shared with him.

She moved to the far right lane and exited I-10. They'd stopped here on their way through the first time. Between the heavy traffic in and out and the available facilities, it was safe enough to stay and rest a while and think. She ignored her own needs and pulled to the curb along the doggie grass. Moe danced on his expandable leash and leaped out when she reached across to open the door. Tethered to her in the car, he tested the length he could run and the speed at which he could get there.

She managed to stop sniffing and rested her head on the wheel. With no one to talk to and no answers in sight, she did the last thing she ever thought she'd do.

Pray.

"OK... *God*. If we've ever spoken, I don't remember, but I think my Aunt Winnie and my mother tried to introduce us when I was little." She ran her wet tissue across the end of her nose and looked around to make sure no one was watching. "I'll get right to the point," she continued and bowed her head. "I need help. I have a mess in Florida. I don't think I was negligent, but I was in charge. I don't see any way out... Then there's my dad. I didn't know it, but he's a terrible person. I don't know what to do with that. I don't think there's enough hours in the day for all the therapy that's going to take. And lastly, God, I love Cole. I think he loves me, too, and I am literally on the road and don't know which way to go. Literally. East or west? I can't go back to Florida because I'll die there. Not physically… but in every other way. And I can't go back to Texas because… because I'm not worthy of the love I found there. I'm not worth what the people there tried to pour into me. I know I'm not good enough. I don't know how to fully love them because my dad saw to it I forgot what my mother and Aunt Winnie showed me. I'm trying my best to remember it. So… that's it. I'm lost." Moe jumped in the car and sent a sloppy lick up the side of her face. "Thank you for listening. Uh… Amen."

The dog leaned over the edge of the passenger seat and nosed his bowl across the floor mat.

"I know. So here's what we're going to do. You're going to eat, I'm going to eat, we're going to take a walk, and I'm going to rest my eyes and my back. And then? I don't know."

But, after a run to a nearby restaurant, the only thing that changed about her situation was the sky. Ominous clouds billowed above her, and fat raindrops smacked the windshield. Large trucks roared nearby on the freeway and the high, halogen lights on the massive parking lot only illuminated the downpour. She moved the car to a well-lit space near the building and pulled Winnie's quilt from the back.

"Cuddle up, Moe. I'm not driving in this. It's really late and I'm tired."

But the dog was squirmier—and stinkier—than usual, and the traffic and road noise kept him in *stalk and growl* mode more than *cuddle and sleep* mode. The packed car made it hard to stretch out and relax, so her rest was short and fitful. Her back ached from the cramped space, and her brain still ached from the turmoil that was her life.

That's why she was so surprised when, after a couple hours of wrestling with Moe, she apparently conked out, slept through the rest of the monsoon, and was jarred awake by her phone's regular alarm.

"Are you kidding me? It's five o'clock in the morning. We slept in our car, pooch. I don't think we've ever done that. It was supposed to be a nap."

Moe stood and did his stretching-shaking thing as she pushed open the dripping door. Knots that formed along her neck and shoulders were slow to ease as she unfurled herself from the front seat and tried to stand. Puddles glistened across the asphalt as water chased more water down the storm drains. Early risers barreled down the freeway with morning traffic and the first sign of light after the rainy night crept into the eastern sky. Birds flew in to peck at trash that had blown from the barrels.

And none of this would have struck her as odd until the robust male cardinal with the slightly damaged crest flew across in front of her and started his morning song from the top of a gazebo on the walking trail. He dropped to the rail and continued to sing as Moe did his best to run through every patch of muddy ground on the property.

Peace and comfort settled around her shoulders and embraced her like a soft, warm blanket made of tangible love. God's love. Winnie's love. Her mother's love.

Now, she had a choice.

She could listen, watch, and believe it was real. She could go with the old story and say it was Winnie who'd come to check on her and her mess of a life and nudge her in the right direction. She could admit God was in it somewhere and it was part of a bigger plan.

She could have faith.

Faith in God, faith in Cole, faith in herself.

Or she could get in her car and drive to Florida.

She'd rather believe.

She stood there for a moment, until a horn blast startled her and set the bird to flight. As she turned, her own words from the video dropped into her head and spirit like a feather dancing and swirling to the ground.

I can do all things through Christ who strengthens me…

I can do all things through Christ who strengthens me…

I. Can Do. All things. Through Christ. Who strengthens. Me.

"Moe! C'mon. I need to make a call."

ෆ๕ஓ

Jacey splashed her way through a sponge bath in the welcome center bathroom. So far, her father hadn't picked up the phone, but she'd keep trying.

"It's so simple, Moe." Her voice bounced off all the metallic doors and the tile floor. "I. Can Do. All things. Through Christ. I don't need anyone else. I don't need my father's approval. Never did. I don't need my old job. I don't technically need Cole, but I want him." She tossed her dirty shirt in her bag and pulled a fresh one over her head. "I don't fully understand how it all works, but I'm starting to get it. If Christ is all I have, I'm still OK. I still have a place in this world. I have a place in Cardinal Point."

The dog gazed at her, completely unimpressed and uninterested.

"Fine. I'm going to stop sharing so much with you." She dusted her cheeks with powder and grabbed the lip balm. "I know it's unhealthy at this point, but if I call Tammy she won't be able to contain herself and will probably be like *well, duh, darlin', I tried to tell you…* and I have talk to Cole in person, so…"

She plucked her bag from a hook on the wall and glanced at the dog who was now clearly trying to escape the conversation by hiding behind on the heavy steel trash can.

"Oh, c'mon."

She sat on a bench near the car and tried her dad again. She shook from the inside out when he picked up. "Daddy?"

"Jacey. I see you've been trying to reach me. I'm at the club."

Of course. Golf on Christmas Eve. Doesn't everyone do that? "I have something to tell you."

"Well?"

"My mother lived."

"What's this about, Jacey? I thought you had news about your case. There are rumors there's been new information. Have you heard from your lawyer?"

"No, and that's not important right now. What's important is that my mother lived. She lived and she was happy. She loved her sister, she loved me, and she loved you. And I know you loved her. And I cannot comprehend why you chose to live as if that didn't happen, or why you chose to force her memory and my Aunt Winnie out of my life, but it doesn't matter. I know now. I know my mother lived and she loved me. And my Aunt Winnie was a wonderful person who lost her only sister and tried to do right by me in her memory. She knew I'd grow up and figure it out and I did. So, you can keep doing your worst if you want to, Daddy, but it no longer applies to me, and you are wasting your time."

She braced for a reaction. A sarcastic retort, a string of curses, but there was oddly nothing. The slight hitch in his breath was the only way she knew he hadn't hung up.

"I need my mother's things," she continued. "I know there is jewelry from my grandparents, and there must be personal items. You need to send those things to me. And I don't know what you did with her ashes, but, if you still have them, I think we need to bury them with the rest of her family in Cardinal Point. Do you understand?"

Still nothing.

"All right, then. I want you to know I love you, Daddy. I should hate you, but I don't. I'll be at my B&B if you need me. I have to go. I have a long drive. I hope you have a Merry Christmas."

She didn't disconnect. She didn't even breathe. After a few seconds, the call was gone.

She opened the car door. "Hop in, Moe. We need to get home."

THIRTEEN

Jacey took the church steps two at a time. An accident on I-10 had added a couple long, grueling hours to her trip home and made her late for church. She'd hoped to swing by the B&B and make herself more presentable, but then realized she had no idea what one wears to storm a church and take back the love of her life—let alone what was appropriate for the Christmas Eve service. Somehow, the holiday shirt Tammy made her for the parade didn't seem like the subtle choice.

So, she slapped on some mascara and left Moe curled up in Winnie's quilt on the front seat while she attended-slash-crashed her first ever Christmas Eve service and attempted to convince Cole not to give up on her.

She paused and rested her head on the heavy, wooden door. Her pulse popped and her emotions whirled. A muffled song from inside the sanctuary floated to her ears. The music was a lot like her life before she came to Cardinal Point—far away and muted—like watching life from behind a plate glass window. Not anymore. Peace and a bone-deep conviction settled over her. She no longer belonged on the outside. Her life was on the other side of the door with her friends and the man she loved. Fortified with that knowledge, she slipped into the back of the church.

An older man smiled and offered her a small white candle. She took it to be polite, but never stopped scanning the dark room for Cole. Somewhere among the crowd of devoted parishioners and anxious children in their Christmas best, he was there, celebrating the true meaning of Christmas.

A dim spotlight illuminated the guy on stage as he sang *Oh, Holy Night*. His voice caressed each note and word, bringing them to life. As the song crescendoed, her soul soared right along with it. In the beauty of the moment, the love of Jesus reached out to her, tempting and sweet. Without thought, without hesitation, she grabbed a hold of that love with both hands. She didn't deserve it, but she'd be crazy to reject such a perfect gift. The tears leaking from her eyes didn't surprise her. She'd accepted the fact that she was now a crier.

When the song changed to *Silent Night*, the congregation stood, and the room began to glow. It started with a single candle then, one by one, each person passed the flame along.

The added light helped her locate Cole. She found him close to the end of a row about six pews in front of her. He stood with Tammy and her family, sandwiched between her best friend and Beth Anne, one of the twins. His dimple flashed when he turn to smile at Tammy and his dark hair gleamed in the candlelight. A jab of uncertainty might have derailed her plans, but she loved this man. He was all she wanted, and nothing would stop her from getting to him.

She made her way to the pew and slipped past the child on his left to stand next to him. When he turned to ignite Beth Anne's candle, he found her instead.

In spite of her best effort, her lips trembled as they worked their way into a smile. "Hi," she whispered, all the while hoping, expecting, and praying he was glad to see her.

"Hey."

"I'm so sorry, Cole." A big, fat tear slid down her face. "I've been a fool and I've hurt you. Please, please forgive me."

Tammy nudged him aside and reached past his lit candle to squeeze her arm. The white fur collar of her Christmas vest partially obscured her face, but didn't hide her huge tears. "Welcome home, darlin'," she said, and then buried her head in her husband's shoulder as if she couldn't handle the emotion of it all.

Candlelight danced in Cole's eyes. He cupped Jacey's face in his free hand and brushed the tear from her cheek, but he didn't say a word.

"Please say something," she begged.

He dropped his hand, furrowed his brow, and tilted his head as if expecting more. Could he not hear her?

He *had* to hear what she said, had to know she was sorry. Music swelled and the voices around them rose in the sweetest melody. Those nearby started to catch on they were having a 'moment' in the middle of church and either tried to ignore them, or step closer to the action.

She didn't care. She'd already waited too long to tell him the truth. She wouldn't wait any longer.

"I said I'm sorry," she practically yelled. "Will you forgive me? I need you to forgive me because I love you, Cole." She stood on her toes to press her face against his and speak into his good ear. "I said I love you, Cole. Do you near me now?"

As her declaration drowned out *Silent Night* in an eight-pew radius, the accompanist played on alone since most people had stopped singing.

Tammy continued to sob against Whit's shoulder.

Cole's emerald eyes crinkled at the corners as a brilliant smile split his face. "I heard you the first time," he said and brought her candle to his. "The *I'm sorry* part I mean. I was waiting for the *I love you* part."

"Well, I love you," she said as he shared the flame. "I love you, I love you, I love you." She glanced at the watching crowd. "I love him," she said and pointed. "Sorry to disturb you all, but I love him."

He bent to kiss her. "I love you, too, Jacey." He pulled her close to him. "I'm so glad you're back," he murmured against her hair.

She smiled up at him. "I'm not back, Cole. I'm home."

ABOUT THE AUTHORS

Jami Crumpton

Born and raised Texas girl, Jami Crumpton, is an award-winning author as well as a wife, mother, and an actress/comedian. *When Love Leads You Home* is her debut inspirational romance. Jami has three adult children and lives north of Houston with her husband of 26 years.

Contact Jami: JamiCrumptonRomance@gmail.com

Carla Rossi

Carla Rossi is a multi-published, award-winning author as well as a cancer survivor, life-long music minister, and speaker. She has been writing inspirational romance since 2007. Carla lives north of Houston with her husband. She has three grown children and two grandchildren. Visit carlarossi.com or amazon.com/author/carlarossi for more of Carla's titles.

Contact Carla:carla@carlarossi.com

Coming soon to Cardinal Point:
Graham and Caroline's story,
The Father-Daughter Picnic

95237376R00121

Made in the USA
Lexington, KY
06 August 2018